HARLEQUIN®
Presents

Enjoy eight new titles from Harlequin Presents in August!

Lucy Monroe brings you her next story in the fabulous ROYAL BRIDES series, and look out for Carole Mortimer's second seductive Sicilian in her trilogy THE SICILIANS. Don't miss Miranda Lee's ruthless millionaire, Sarah Morgan's gorgeous Greek tycoon, Trish Morey's Italian boss and Jennie Lucas's forced bride! Plus, be sure to read Kate Hardy's story of passion leading to pregnancy in *One Night, One Baby,* and the fantastic *Taken by the Maverick Millionaire* by Anna Cleary!

We'd love to hear what you think about Presents. E-mail us at Presents@hmb.co.uk or join in the discussions at www.iheartpresents.com and www.sensationalromance.blogspot.com, where you'll also find more information about books and authors!

RED HOT REVENGE

There are times in a man's life...

when only seduction will settle old scores!

Pick up our exciting series of revenge-filled
romances—they're recommended and red-hot!

Available only from Harlequin Presents®

Trish Morey

THE ITALIAN BOSS'S MISTRESS OF REVENGE

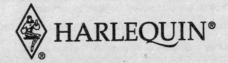

HARLEQUIN®

TORONTO • NEW YORK • LONDON
AMSTERDAM • PARIS • SYDNEY • HAMBURG
STOCKHOLM • ATHENS • TOKYO • MILAN • MADRID
PRAGUE • WARSAW • BUDAPEST • AUCKLAND

ISBN-13: 978-0-373-12751-1
ISBN-10:   0-373-12751-0

THE ITALIAN BOSS'S MISTRESS OF REVENGE

First North American Publication 2008.

Copyright © 2008 by Trish Morey.

www.eHarlequin.com

Printed in U.S.A.

All about the author…
Trish Morey

TRISH MOREY wrote her first book at age eleven for a children's book-week competition. Entitled *Island Dreamer,* it proved to be her first rejection. Shattered and broken, she turned to a life where she could combine her love of fiction with her need for creativity—and became a chartered accountant. Life wasn't all dull, though, as she embarked on a skydiving course, completing three jumps before deciding that she'd given her fear of heights a run for its money.

Meanwhile, she fell in love and married a handsome guy who cut computer code. After the birth of their second daughter, Trish spied an article saying that Harlequin was actively seeking new authors. It was one of those "Eureka!" moments—Trish was going to be one of those authors!

Eleven years after reading that fateful article, the magical phone call came, and Trish finally realized her dream. According to Trish, writing and selling a book is a major life achievement that ranks right up there with jumping out of an airplane and motherhood. All three take commitment, determination and sheer guts, but the effort is so very, very worthwhile.

Trish now lives with her husband and four young daughters in a special part of South Australia, surrounded by orchards and bushland and visited by the occasional koala and kangaroo.

You can visit Trish at her Web site at www.trishmorey.com, or drop her a line at trish@trishmorey.com.

To my big sister, Toni.
Congratulations on achieving your half-century!
Happy birthday, Sis. Here's to the next 50 years
With much love,
Trish
XXX

CHAPTER ONE

I<small>T WAS</small> a filthy night. Which suited Dante Carrazzo's filthy mood right down to the ground.

The BMW's windscreen wipers struggled to keep pace with the blinding rain, while its headlights picked out little more in the night fog than the ghostly shadows of gum trees looming claw-like over the unfamiliar Adelaide Hills road. If there was a boutique-hotel anywhere in the area, it sure didn't want to be found.

Which was probably no surprise, given his plans for it.

He steered the car tight around another bend, his frustration mounting as his headlights met nothing other than their own reflection over a slick ribbon of road disappearing into the gloom.

Tiredness tugged at his senses and stung his eyes, eight hours behind the wheel after a full day's battling to bring the Quinn deal to fruition starting to take its toll. Dante clamped down on the weakness the same way he did any other, forcing himself to alertness. It had been a long time, but he knew this was the right road. It had to be here, hidden under this blanket of fog, somewhere...

He was past the poorly lit turn-off before he realized it.

With a muttered curse, he wheeled the car around at the first opportunity and headed back, pulling the car into the long driveway and towards the distant, eerie glow of lights that heralded his destination.

Ashton House.

At last.

Shrouded in swirling mist, the old mansion turned boutique-hotel looked almost sinister, its windows dark and unwelcoming, the old sandstone walls glowing unnaturally in the muted lantern light. He parked the car, mentally adding to his description the words, "brooding" and "resentful".

Almost as if it hated him just as much as he hated every last thing it represented.

So be it.

The fog wrapped around him as he stepped from the car, icy droplets stinging his skin. He pulled his bag from the car and strode the few feet to the arched entrance-lobby, leaning against the night bell as he swiped the dampness from his coat. He waited precisely ten seconds before pressing it again.

'I have a reservation,' he said, brushing past the open-mouthed night clerk into the warm interior the second the door finally opened.

Behind him he heard the massive timber-panelled door being shut, closing out the swirling mist and cold. 'I'll certainly check for you, sir,' said the clerk, making his way to the polished timber reception-counter. 'Although I'm afraid we seem to have a full house tonight.'

Dante fixed the clerk with a stare that would splinter rocks. 'I hope that doesn't mean you've given my room away.'

The clerk frowned, his eyes flicking nervously away to his screen. 'It will only take a moment to check, sir. What name did you say?'

'I didn't. And it's Carrazzo. Dante Carrazzo.'

'Ah!' The clerk straightened as if someone had shoved an iron rod up his spine. Dante caught the smell of fear that came with it. It came as no surprise. All of the staff would be wondering—now that he owned Ashton House lock, stock and barrel—exactly what it was he had in mind for it. All of them would be on tenterhooks.

He allowed himself a wry smile. Given his reputation, they had a right to be.

'We…we weren't expecting you tonight, not with all the Melbourne airports closed.'

'Do you have a room for me or not?' His eyes were stinging again, indigestion burning his stomach. After the day and night he'd had, what he needed right now was a few hours of precious sleep, not a discussion about his travel arrangements. And if they'd given away his room…

'I'm sorry. Of course, sir,' the night clerk blustered, passing a pen for Dante to sign the register, while at the same time reaching for the room key. 'Your suite was held. It's just that we didn't expect you until morning.'

'Last time I looked,' he replied smoothly, his voice modulated to low while every word was aimed like a barb, 'it *was* morning. Now, what time will the manager be here?'

'Mac—Mackenzi will be on from seven.'

'Good,' he said, scribbling his signature on the registration form. 'Have this Mackenzi meet me in the restaurant at nine. Now, remind me where I can find this suite…'

The clerk gave him directions as soon as Dante had

convinced him he was capable of carrying his own luggage. But he'd barely started down the passageway before he heard his name.

He turned on a sigh, impatient and unimpressed. 'What is it?'

The clerk shrank noticeably in response, as if already wishing he could take back his interruption. 'I meant to tell you, Mr Carrazzo, the staff organized a welcome package for you. You'll find it waiting in your suite. But please, don't hesitate to let me know if there's anything else you need.'

'Oh, don't worry,' he growled, 'I will.' He turned and made his way down the old stone-walled billiards room, and through the passageway that led to the wing where the presidential suite took up half the space. If the staff really believed something as insignificant as a welcome package was going to change his mind about this place, then they were in for a major disappointment.

The plush carpet absorbed his footfall. The hotel slept silently around him, the only sound the burst of rain against the roof signalling the end of the brief respite, while the distant roll of thunder promised still more bad weather to come.

Weariness dragged at him now, muting the feeling of triumph that had come with learning Ashton House was his. He paused and took a breath, the key lodged deep into the timber double-doors that marked the entry to his suite—the same suite that Jonas and Sara Douglas had shared seventeen years ago.

Seventeen years it had taken him to get here.

Seventeen years, and now the last asset, the jewel in the

crown of the Douglas Property Group, was finally his. That deserved some kind of celebratory toast, surely?

The door swung open to a dimly lit corridor as the heavens really opened above, the noise from the rain now a deafening roar. The bedroom lay to the left, he seemed to recall, so instead he turned to the right, remembering a sitting room, snapping on the lights and immediately dimming them down low. He dropped his bag and opened a timber sideboard. *Bingo.* He emptied two tiny bottles into a tumbler and took a swig, rolling the malt whiskey around his tongue before tossing it back, appreciating the burst of fire all the way down to his belly. He sighed an appreciative sigh. He'd needed that.

A few seconds later and he'd shrugged out of his jacket and reefed out his shirt, unbuttoning his sleeves as he circled the room. Unexpectedly, it wasn't at all cold in the suite, despite the two walls where uncovered French windows looked out into foggy rain-streaked blankness. Another wall held a door that he remembered led to the bathroom and connected with the bedroom beyond—and a bed that beckoned.

Could he sleep in a room that had once housed Sara and Jonas?

Oh, hell, yes! It would be nothing more than the sweet, satisfying taste of revenge that would fuel his dreams tonight.

He finished in the bathroom, leaving his clothes where they fell noiselessly under the hammer of rain on the roof, and stepped naked into the bedroom.

And *that* was when he found her.

CHAPTER TWO

THE NAKED SKIN of lean shoulder-blades glowed pearlescent under the wash of light angling from the bathroom door, while copper-lit mahogany hair flowed in waves across the pillow. Her face was turned away, but even shadows couldn't hide the fine line of her jaw or the sweep of long lashes over high cheekbones.

Some welcome package, he thought with reluctant appreciation, muscle weariness morphing into testosterone-fuelled interest in an instant. He moved closer to the bed. By rights, *his* bed.

He had to hand it to the staff here, they were nothing if not creative. Nowhere else had the personnel tried the Goldilocks approach, trying to soften his attitude by pressing a little tender flesh onto him. And that flesh did look tender, he mused. Tender, smooth and very inviting.

Not that he was really interested. No-one decided who Dante Carrazzo slept with. And no whore was about to change his mind about what he had planned for this place. She would just have to find herself another bed to warm tonight. It shouldn't take her long, given her obvious attributes.

He was about to rouse her when he caught sight of

himself and cursed. In this state, he'd never convince her that her services weren't required.

Wrapped in one of the white hotel-robes from the closet, he reached once again for her shoulder, just as a clap of thunder shook the room, the curtained windows lighting up a scant second later. She stirred and murmured, and he thought his job already done, but she merely rolled over, sinking back into oblivion on a sigh.

Breath hissed through his teeth as his eyes drank in the new, improved view. Even with her eyes closed she was some temptress, her lips full and inviting. But it was the cream-skinned breasts topped with dusky nipples that shook his resolve, nipples he could see were already firming with their exposure to the air.

Not the only things around here firming.

Heat targeted his groin, ramping up the pressure to an ache, and relaying the message that he was now way, way overdressed. What had been before no more than a general but suppressible interest in the fairer sex, had combusted into something much more carnal. Much more necessary. What would it take to wake her up? If she could sleep through a storm like this, it might take a while to wake her by conventional methods.

Which left him with the unconventional.

He made a sound like a growl. Maybe he had been too hasty, wanting to dispose of her so soon. It wasn't like he was about to change his mind about this place, but he was due a celebration. What better place to have it than in the very room where Jonas and Sara had lain the night before they'd smiled like sharks and had told him the truth?

Pain, savage and raw, sliced through him at the memories,

turning to bile in his throat, as if it had only been yesterday and not all those years ago.

Damn them! He would bury every part of their memory, every part of their legacy, just as he buried himself deep inside this woman.

Then he would toss her out.

He returned to the bathroom, locating what he needed before dispensing with the robe. Now it was time to find out just how difficult his Goldilocks would be to rouse. The more difficult the better, he acknowledged. For tonight he didn't want conversation.

Tonight was all about retribution.

She was still on her back when he returned, her face to one side, her arms flung wide, her perfect breasts exposed for the taking. *His* taking. He took a moment to drink her in. The face was almost angelic in repose, while the naked form of a goddess called to him like a siren. He took in the twin globes of her breasts, and the shapely dip to her waist, and what lay lower, hidden for now by the covers, but hinting at more hidden treasures. If he wasn't mistaken, her lower end was just as bare as her top—and, if he'd had any doubt that his surprise visitor wasn't intended for his pleasure, the fact she lay there naked removed any such doubt in a heartbeat. So, she was into saving time? He appreciated such little economies, especially tonight.

He dragged in a sudden burst of air, and needed to balance the weight of blood pooling in his groin. He was glad she hadn't awakened when that clap of thunder had rent the skies. This way would be much more entertaining. 'And much more satisfying,' he murmured as he gently knelt down on the bed alongside her.

She barely stirred, even when he pushed a wayward coil of hair from her face. Unable to resist a further touch, he ran the back of one finger down one shadowed cheek and was rewarded by the merest hint of a sigh, her lips parting as she drew in air, lifting her chest and doing amazing things to those breasts.

His gaze lingered there, taking in the creamy glow of her skin and the pebbled peaks of her breasts, calling to him now like beacons. He would answer that call, but there was no rush, and right now he hadn't finished with her mouth.

With the pad of one thumb, he gently traced the outline of her lips, feeling her warm breath against his skin, taking her murmur of pleasure as a sign of encouragement.

He dipped his head, drinking in the warm, feminine scent of her skin before giving her mouth the briefest of passes. She sighed, her head rolling to one side. He brushed her lips with his own, finding them warm and welcoming. She moved under his mouth, even in sleep finding that sweet spot where their lips meshed perfectly, inviting him to linger, inviting him to explore further.

Reluctantly he pulled away, watching her shadowed face as her body reacted to what he was doing, looking for any hint of her wakefulness but finding none. It was different, he realized, pleasuring a woman asleep, different and more arousing. There was something more evocative, more empowering.

Sex by stealth.

He allowed himself a smile as his hand found her shoulder, cupping it, enjoying the contrast of toned flesh and bone under his hand as his mouth once again met hers. Even in sleep her movements mimicked his, wanting to participate, trying to hold on longer to the fantasy. His tongue traced the line of her mouth, and she shuddered beneath him, turning the kiss electric. 'Oh, yes,' she gasped into his mouth on a sigh.

Her breathing was quickening, and he lifted his head, half-surprised at the jolt he'd just experienced, half-expecting that first flicker of wakefulness, because he knew she'd felt it too. But still it didn't come, despite the firmed breasts and jutting nipples, despite the noticeable shallow hitch to her breathing. She was dreaming about sex, he could tell, imagining a lover who visited deep in the night and made her every wish come true.

He growled and gave a smile. Only too soon she would open those eyes and discover he was real. What colour would those eyes be? he wondered absently as he ran his fingertips along the curve of her collarbone. Brown, he decided, his fingers dipping into the space between them. They would have to be brown with her colouring. His hand made the return journey, his fingers spread wider this time so that his thumb scooped across the rise of her breasts.

This time she moaned, arching her back and shifting fractionally in her sleep, sending her bed clothes lower, exposing a hint of curvy waist above the sensual flare of hips. Honey-smooth skin, gleaming in the lowlight. His mouth went dry. Even asleep and unknowing she was an invitation. How much more so would she be when awake?

The ache in his groin turned more insistent, more demanding, the beast alive, wanting and hungry. Then she murmured something—a name, almost an entreaty. *Richard?*

Suddenly his little game lost appeal. Half of him wanted to take his time and play this game for all it was worth, to explore every curve and hollow of her flesh, to savour the secret pleasure while he waited for her to awaken, but the other half of him craved release. Release, followed by blessed sleep. The last thing he wanted was her thinking of someone else while he made love to her. He wanted her awake. He wanted her to realize just who it was making love to her, and then he'd proceed to obliterate every trace of 'Richard' from her memory.

And there would be time enough to explore later. Now it was time for business. His fingers scooped down her chest. Right now her breasts were at the top of his agenda.

'Time you woke up, Goldilocks,' he said, before his mouth descended on one perfect nipple.

The dream was back. Her night caller was here again—the one who spoke to Mackenzi not with words but with heated lips and sweet caresses, the dark stranger who drugged her with sensuality and reassured her that she was desirable and warm and all woman. The one who made her want to believe it.

And tonight he seemed more persuasive, more convincing and more real than ever.

But it was a dream—it was always a dream—and she knew the rules; that if she opened her eyes her dream lover would vanish and it would be over. And yet for just a dream her senses were buzzing, her pulse racing, and she wished more than anything that for once it was more than just a dream—because tonight she felt like a real woman, and because she wanted to believe, more than anything, what he was telling her.

So, so much!

She felt his fingers stroking her hair and her face, setting her skin tingling. She felt his lips pressed gently on her own, she even imagined she could feel his warm breath on her face.

So real.

So real that, she wondered, would tonight be the night? Or would her dream lover flee once more before the dawn and leave her tossing and turning, damp and slickened with sweat, yet still unfulfilled, and doubting herself more than ever?

And, worst of all, believing that what Richard had told her must be true.

That she was no kind of lover at all.

That she was frigid.

She drifted then, on a sea of sensation and unearthly pleasures, wondering vaguely why her mystery lover would return for a repeat performance if she was, wondering why only he seemed to unleash such unfamiliar passion in her. She sizzled inside now, as her mystery lover's lips moved over hers, and heat became electric as she felt the dart of moist flesh zip from one side of her mouth to the other. She trembled under the caress, imagining that this time she could even taste him, while she willed his attentions on further. Further south. Where her need was building in an increasingly desperate ache.

If he could make her tremble like that by nothing more than a mere touch of his lips, what more could he do by moving his attention to other, more demanding locations?

She gave herself up to the sensations spiralling down her body, the sensual drug taking control as a familiar unfairness echoed once more through her senses. *Richard.* How was it that he had never elicited anywhere near such a physical response in her as her dream lover? Had it really been all her fault?

And then nothing mattered—not Richard, or her questions or her self-doubts. Her heart was beating so loudly now, her pulse a sensual drumbeat that turned to a throb deep down inside and drowned out such plaguing thoughts. If her dream lover could make her feel so good, so real, even just for the moment, then who cared? Not her. She just wanted to enjoy for as long as it lasted.

Sound outside her heartbeat interrupted her thoughts— a voice, and words that made no sense, tumbling together into fairy tales and nonsense—and then all was silent apart from her groan as she felt his tongue circle her nipple, sending flaming arrows deep down inside. From somewhere in the passion-blinded recesses of her mind it occurred to her: her dream lover had never spoken before, not with words.

Fear shimmied up her spine as she pushed away at the remnants of sleep, still at war with herself, torn between not wanting to do anything to banish her dream lover, and yet knowing that this time was different—that tonight something was majorly out of step.

Jagged lightning hastened her ascent, and she opened her eyes to a booming roll of thunder that made the building shake around her. Yet it was nothing compared to the thunderclap of finding his dark head at her breast.

It wasn't a dream! The sensual web that had wound itself around her while she'd slept was no figment of her imagination, her arousal no fantasy. This man—and what he was doing to her—was shockingly real.

She cried out something garbled and panicked, jerking

herself away, her hands reaching for the bed clothes and dragging them higher.

'Good morning, Goldilocks, I was beginning to think you'd never wake up.' His voice soothed, even as what felt like a steel band clamped around her, anchoring her to the bed. But she couldn't have moved a muscle, even if she'd tried, not when another bolt of lightning lit up the room and the face of her dream lover with it.

A moment of frozen shock turned into a chill of abject horror, for even after the lightning had passed and the room plunged back into darkness, the lines and planes of the face hovering close remained boldly etched in her mind's eye. The lines and planes of a face she knew only too well.

'Dante!'

The very man with the power of life and death over the hotel. The very man she'd sworn to fight tooth and nail to ensure he wouldn't destroy this property and the livelihoods of all who worked within it.

It hadn't been a dream.

And the reality was far, far worse.

It was a nightmare.

He gave what looked in the gloom like a predatory smile, full of dark meaning and sinful intent, and she felt her insides lurch. He touched the back of the fingers of one hand to her cheek and against her better judgement it was all she could do not to lean into his electric touch. 'I never would have guessed,' he said cryptically, before unhooking the arm holding her prisoner and reaching for something on the bedside table. The spell broken, Mackenzi took the opportunity to back away across the mattress, clutching the bed clothes to breasts still too-acutely tingling after his tongue's ministrations. She squeezed her eyes shut. *Oh God, that had been Dante Carrazzo's tongue!*

'I...I should be going,' she stammered, still trying to come to terms with what he was doing here so early, and cursing herself for taking the easy option of making use of his vacant room rather than dragging a pull-out bed to the laundry. But even harder to come to terms with was how any man, least of all *him*, could have had that effect on her and made her feel so alive, so aroused.

And then she heard the rip of foil and he turned back with something in his hands, and she discovered in a rush of awareness something new about her late-night visitor— that, from what little light there was in the room, the gleam of his muscled torso told her he was, like her, completely and utterly naked. Her gaze moved lower and she swallowed, her tongue tied, her brain scrambled, forgetting everything in the rush of hormones that flooded her system.

Hormones she wasn't supposed to have.

Hormones that wanted to leap from her skin when she watched in fascination as he rolled the condom along his long length. It was dark in the room, but even the shadows couldn't disguise the dimensions being sheathed. How would that feel inside her? she wondered dry-mouthed as every bit of moisture in her body headed south. If indeed it were possible. And suddenly, inexplicably, *insanely*, she wanted more than anything to find out.

'You don't want to leave now,' he assured her, taking advantage of her confusion when he'd finished his task to gather her in his arms, and leaving her to wonder whether now he'd taken to reading her mind. 'Not when we're only just getting to the main event.'

Even if she'd wanted to, she doubted she could have moved. Her body acted of its own volition, resisting any and all attempts to protect herself from his advances—especially when he dipped his head towards her breasts, his lips latching onto a nipple. She gasped, giving into temptation while battling to locate logical thought. *This is a bad idea*, she seemed to register from somewhere under the battery of sensations that accompanied his suckling. A very bad idea. But for the life of her she couldn't work out why.

Not such a bad idea after all, another sinful voice crooned, *if finally you get to experience what Richard's been telling you you're incapable of. And where's the danger?* the voice argued. *It's dark, he'll be asleep in five minutes, and he'll never even know it's you.*

He'll never know it's you.

The words echoed in her head like a mantra and she tried to keep hold of it, to believe it. She had to believe it. Because she'd reached the point of no return. Now there was no going back, no escape, even if she wanted to. She didn't want to.

His hand ran down her side, tracing the curve of her hip and the outside line of her leg, and she shuddered into his touch. Then he turned at her knee and started the slow, sensual trip back along the inside. She pressed her head back into the bed. Had anyone ever died of anticipation? When his hand found her curls and lingered there, combing her lazily with his fingers, she could believe it. When he parted her and found that tightly wired centre of her existence, jolting her like an electric shock, she could almost believe she had.

'Please,' she urged, not sure what she was asking for, just that it be mercifully quick.

His heated mouth moved to her throat, nuzzling below her ear and turning her spine along with her defences to liquid. So it was no wonder that her legs fell open when he levered himself up and positioned himself between them.

Later she knew she would be shocked by her complicity, but what choice did she have? If only it didn't feel so good, she told herself. If only it didn't feel so right. But how could she fight what felt so essentially good? And how could she fight what seemed so essential?

It was as if her dream lover had come to life and had stayed to beckon her on, even after she'd opened her eyes. It was as if her every wish for sexual gratification had come true. She was too far gone, too fuelled by a sensuous dream that had primed her senses to within a fraction of release, her body already hell-bent on a course that demanded completion, a completion drawing deliciously closer by the second.

He nudged, poised against her opening, and her whole being focused on that one spot, that one sensation, where her muscles instinctively tightened to draw him in. She reached for him then, unable to pretend she was uninvolved, that this was merely something happening to her. For she was part of this too. Hot and smooth, skin had never felt so delicious, and it was impossible to resist running her hands down his toned sides to his flanks, drinking in the heat through her palms, testing the firmness of his tight buttocks with her fingers.

He groaned against her throat, and gave a thrust of his hips that sent him surging into her. So this was how it felt, she thought, as every nerve ending in her body lurched with the thrill, every muscle focused on accommodating him; this was what it should be like.

He pulled away, and she wanted to cry out with the sense of loss, but he returned on another stroke, pressing deeper, giving her more of him. She accepted hungrily, a delicious pressure mounting inside her, and each successive thrust taking him further until he was planted deep inside. He paused then, and if that had been the end of it it would have been enough, the sensations he'd awakened in her already too many and too wondrous to catalogue. But he started to move again, to rock back and forth, setting up a rhythm, a delicious friction. She angled her hips up to receive him, as if it were possible to take him deeper still, using muscles she'd never known she had, making moves she hadn't known she knew, feeling things she hadn't known possible to feel.

Already she wanted to cry out in exhilaration for all she felt, and still he was taking her higher.

Her hands clung to his chest, clung to heated skin now slick with sweat, against chest hair that coiled possessively around her fingers, against a nipple that intruded tight into her palm as his heartbeat thumped out a song to lure her in. She tossed her head from side to side as he continued the onslaught, leaving her gasping for air as her senses seemed determined to spiral out of control.

But instead of oxygen the air she breathed was filled with the scent of him, the testosterone-laden notes intoxicating, compelling, compounding the experience until he was everywhere—inside her, around her, in the air she breathed.

His pace was frantic, her own need building with it, having no choice but to go with the forces spiralling inside her. He dropped his head to one breast and took a nipple deep into his mouth, suckling on it tightly and triggering what felt like lightning bolts inside her. Her back arched and her fingers lodged tight in his skin, the combination of excruciating pleasure and exquisite pain connecting with the delicious fullness between her thighs, completing the circuit.

She came apart like the force of a sky rocket, exploding into myriad tiny stars that sparkled and shone and floated on the breeze as they drifted back down to earth.

He followed her, pumping his release with a roar that sounded like a cry of victory, before collapsing alongside her on the bed.

She dragged up the sheet and lay there panting, staring up at the darkened ceiling, disbelief uppermost in her mind. Disbelief that someone who'd been told she was frostier than the polar ice-caps could have burned up so completely with a stranger. Disbelief that that stranger should be none other than Dante Carrazzo.

Fear zipped down her spine. Now that she'd been satisfied, now that she'd given into her body's desperate desires, there was no place for her mind to hide, no place for her fear.

What the hell had she done?

She squeezed her eyes closed, clamping one hand over her mouth to prevent her from crying out in distress. What had she been thinking? How could she have allowed anyone—especially him—to do *that* to her?

But there'd been no room for thinking, no room for logic, not with the bevy of sensations he'd triggered off inside her. Even now her muscles still hummed, as if clinging onto the memories of unfamiliar passion. Unfamiliar yet very welcome passion.

Would she have done anything differently if she'd had her time over? She doubted it. She dragged in a breath, sorting out her options.

He'll never know it's you. The words of her mantra came back to her. She stole a sideways look at him. Oh no, it wasn't as simple as that. Dante Carrazzo *couldn't* recognize her—or her cause was doomed even before she'd started.

She sensed the subtle change in him that she hoped signalled sleep. She turned her head as the digital clock behind him flicked over to three a.m., the light from the display casting a red glow on his outline, making him look even more ruthless than she knew him to be, the chiselled line of his jaw hard and uncompromising, his mouth set and unyielding.

Unlike before...

She waited a few moments more, listening to the steady rhythm of his breathing and assuring herself he was really asleep, before easing herself from the bed, gathering up the pile of folded clothes she'd left on an armchair and bolting from the room.

Oh no. She would *not* think about how amazing that mouth had felt on her skin.

She would *not!*

CHAPTER THREE

HE WAS ALREADY waiting for her, seated in a private alcove at the far side of the busy restaurant, his attitude bearing all the hallmarks of one reputed to be so ruthless in business, his expression grim and with a jaw that looked as if it was used to being permanently clenched. Even so, there was a something about him that kept female heads around him turning. It wasn't that he was classically handsome under that dark scowl, with too many strong angles, too many shadowed recesses, and too little compassion marking his features. It was more a kind of terrible beauty that he wore, a smouldering intensity. Compelling. Dangerous.

Just looking at him was enough to make Mackenzi's internal muscles clench involuntarily with memories of how that smouldering intensity had felt inside her. Dante Carrazzo was the most striking man in the restaurant, exuding power in every movement and impatient gesture—and thinking about how he'd filled her so completely just a few short hours ago…

Mackenzi tried to ignore the sick feeling roiling through her gut and smoothed her palms down her skirt, telling herself for the hundredth time that he'd never recognize her. Not with her clothes on. And with her hair up, and her reading glasses perched defensively on her nose, she must look radically different. Besides, it had been dark in the suite, and he'd been far more interested in getting his rocks off than being bothered with introductions.

What the hell kind of man did something like that anyway—launched himself on a sleeping woman like he had a God-given right to have sex with her? She might have been sleeping in the bed reserved for him, but he hadn't been expected to arrive for hours, and she certainly didn't recall tattooing 'take me' on her forehead before she'd gone to sleep.

She swallowed back on her guilt. Just because she hadn't backed away when she'd had the chance, didn't make it right. And just because she'd enjoyed it didn't make it right. He'd taken advantage of the situation, and of her.

A couple emerged from the lift behind, making their way past her into the busy restaurant, reminding her that she should be doing likewise. Standing in the doorway was no way to save the hotel. A deep breath later, her face schooled into cool professionalism, she once again clamped down on the fear that threatened to turn her stomach.

He wouldn't recognize her. He couldn't...

The *maître d'* threw her a worried frown as she entered the buzzing room, mouthing the warning, 'Table one,' and flicking his head in Dante's direction as she passed. She forced a thin smile and nodded, knowing the staff needed her to be confident and strong right now, rather than a weak-kneed woman who'd just been bedded by the boss. A pity that was exactly how she felt.

She stopped close to the table where he sat flicking impatiently through the business pages. Beyond him the picture windows revealed nothing but a wall of white as fog still held the hotel prisoner. Right now it felt like that same fog had shrink-wrapped her lungs. Oh God, how the hell was she supposed to do this?

'Mr Carrazzo.'

He tossed a careless glance in her direction before glancing down at his watch, and then turning his attention back to the paper. 'I've already ordered.'

'You asked for a meeting, Mr Carrazzo,' she ventured, trying to keep the tremor from both her voice and her fingers as she held out her hand to him. 'Mackenzi Keogh.'

This time the look he gave her took much longer, the appraisal much more thorough, and Mackenzi felt her cheeks begin to flare as his eyes lingered on her face, a slight frown creasing his brow.

'You're Mackenzi?' he asked, without taking her hand.

'That's right.'

'You're a woman.'

She raised an eyebrow, half-tempted to tell him he'd well and truly discovered that fact already. Instead she dropped her hand, grateful beyond belief that he hadn't taken it—and that she hadn't been subjected to the warm press of his flesh once more—and let go an uncharacteristic retort. 'That's right. At least, last time I checked I was.' And she proceeded to slide into the chair opposite.

He scowled at her as a waitress appeared, curtailing conversation as she poured Mackenzi a coffee before topping up his. And Dante continued to regard her while she busied herself arranging and then rearranging her napkin in her lap, steadfastly avoiding his gaze as she declined an invitation to order breakfast. Nothing was going to sit comfortably in her stomach today, but the coffee might at least lend her strength.

'What kind of name is Mackenzi for a woman?'

'It's *my* name, Mr Carrazzo,' she answered, still edgy, but for the first time daring to look him anywhere near in the eye, her confidence edging upwards. If he hadn't recognized her yet, then maybe, just maybe, he never would. After all, she'd hardly been a face to him last night—merely a service-provider. 'And I presume,' she continued, 'you didn't arrange this meeting to discuss the merits or otherwise of my parents' choice.'

Not many things surprised Dante Carrazzo. Not any more. But Ashton House had already provided him with a hat trick of surprises. First had been the discovery of the welcome package warming his bed, the woman who'd ensured him a rapid and very satisfied descent into sleep.

Second had been her absence this morning. Sure, he'd been intending to throw her out anyway, but it had grated that she'd been the one to leave before he'd really had a chance to determine when he was finished with her. Surely a welcome package should hang around until she'd outlived her welcome?

But he'd woken this morning and found nothing more than her scent imprinted on his pillow and a need for her in his loins that had had to go unsatisfied.

And now yet another surprise—a manager with a man's name and an attitude that wavered between acute edginess one minute and open hostility the next. He'd been expecting the latter, he was well used to it, but he'd also been expecting the same smell of fear that the night clerk had radiated. Yet the way she'd blushed when he'd looked at her, and then plucked at her napkin like an adolescent on her first date rather than meet his gaze across the table, was something different.

By rights she should be fearful. Surely she realized how vulnerable her position was? He sipped his coffee, all the time weighing her up, trying to put his finger on exactly what it was about her that struck him as not quite right. She sat shifting in her chair, her eyes never quite meeting his, her teeth plucking at her lower lip like she was uncomfortable in the pause. *Good.*

Silence could be useful like that, telling you more about a person than when they spoke. Like her body was telling him right now. So she was uncomfortable when he looked at her—why was that? Most women had no problem with his perusal—most welcomed it, many more invited it.

And she must be used to men looking at her. She was really no hardship to look at, even in her mousy little manager's outfit. She had pleasant enough features; maybe her nose was a little crooked, but there were curves under that corporate shirt that hinted at some kind of promise.

She made a small sound in the back of her throat, and he unapologetically adjusted his gaze higher. 'Mr Carrazzo,' she ventured cautiously, staring from behind her glasses at a point somewhere over his shoulder. 'I've taken the liberty of pencilling in a ten-thirty a.m. meeting with the staff to outline what plans you have for Ashton House, but in the meantime, perhaps you might permit me to summarize some of the staff's concerns?'

He gave a brief nod, still more interested in what it was

about this woman that bothered him than any pointless attempts at getting him to change his mind.

'Ashton House is the premiere hotel accommodation in the Adelaide Hills,' she began. 'A boutique-hotel, whose roots go back to the mid-eighteen hundreds. Here we employ fifty staff, all of whom are now anxious to know where their jobs stand. More than anxious given the way you've seen fit to close at least half of the other properties you've acquired in the last two years. Naturally, the staff is nervous. They need to know if they have a future here, and for that they need an assurance that Ashton House will be retained by you as a boutique-hotel.'

'Is there any particular reason why I should keep it?'

Mackenzi blinked, clearly thrown by his question. 'Because it's worth it. Nothing else in the Adelaide Hills, probably in all of Adelaide, comes close.'

'Why?' he demanded, already bored. 'What is it that brings people here?'

'The beauty of the district, for a start,' she countered. 'The views…'

He turned his gaze pointedly to the expanse of windows beside them, where nothing existed but a swirling world of white. 'Oh yes,' he mocked. 'I can understand that.'

She slumped back in her chair and he smiled. She'd dropped herself into that one and she knew it. Maybe that was what her nervousness was about—she was just completely out of her depth, too inexperienced to know what it felt like to have the rug pulled out from under your feet. In which case this experience could only benefit her.

He took a sip of his coffee, already satisfied he would

meet little opposition with his current plans, and turned his attention back to the article he'd been reading.

'Mr Carrazzo.'

He looked up, half-surprised she hadn't already scampered off somewhere to nurse her shaky nerves and bruised ego.

'If you don't mind me saying, the staff has a right to know what the future holds for their jobs. They need to know, now that you've taken possession of Ashton House, exactly what you have planned for it.'

His breakfast arrived and he bided his time, letting the tense-looking waitress place his plate just so, grinding on pepper, and topping up his coffee. On the waitress he could sense the familiar fear, the overwhelming need to please and then get the hell away from him. So why not on the woman sitting opposite—who appeared to be all fire and sparks one minute, nervous like a schoolgirl the next?

'I own Ashton House,' he said, injecting his voice with more than a hint of menace. 'I can do with it whatever I damn well please.'

He watched her chest swell on a breath as she sat up ramrod straight, her hands clasped tightly together on the table. 'Like you've done with those others you've acquired?'

'Those properties are hardly your concern.'

'But what you've done with them is! Three perfectly good businesses destroyed, three hotels gutted and turned into apartment blocks. And all for what?'

Revenge, he thought, rolling the word around like he was savouring it. *How sweet it is.* But he didn't expect anyone else to understand. Nobody else could. Nobody else had been to that black hole he'd been thrust into and had had to clamber his way out of, one bleeding hand over the other. 'That's progress,' he tossed off casually. 'The world moves on.'

'And is that the kind of progress you have in mind for Ashton House? Are you planning for the world to "move on" here too—so you can fill up the world with more of your precious apartment blocks?'

Dante put his knife and fork down deliberately before taking another sip of his coffee, contemplating her over the rim of his cup. Her colour was up again, the chest below her shirt rising and falling rapidly, and once again he had the feeling there was something he was missing.

Or was it just that she was the first person he'd met along this journey who hadn't moved out of his way and bowed to the inevitable? He would never have expected such impassioned argument from someone who'd looked so meek and nervous when she'd first appeared.

'Not an option,' he said, shrugging off that line of thought, and getting back to her question in the next breath. 'The local council here would never approve it.'

'Which means you've considered it, then!'

It was an accusation rather than a question, but he ignored the jibe. He hadn't come here to make friends with anyone, and he didn't care what anyone thought. It was far too late for that. 'As it happens, I have an entirely different fate in mind for Ashton House.'

'What does that mean exactly?' Her eyes narrowed. 'Do you plan to keep Ashton House going after all?'

Despite her cautious words, he could see the hope lining her features, hope that he knew would be tragically short-lived. He leaned back low in his chair, his hands finding his pockets as a smile of satisfaction tugged at the corners of his mouth. He'd achieved almost everything he'd set out to do just seventeen short years ago, and the proximity to his goal was like a drug fuelling his bloodstream. Now there was just one final act.

He couldn't think about it without smiling. 'I'm going to destroy it,' he told her. 'I'm going to pull out every window and every door and then leave it to the elements to moulder, until it's nothing more than a crumbling ruin.'

Shock exploded inside her, wrenching away her voice, so that when it came it was more breath than voice, a whisper that felt like she'd swallowed sandpaper. 'Why would you do that?'

'Because I can.'

His voice was cold as ice, his eyes devoid of life. No, Mackenzi realized, shaking her head with disbelief at his callous announcement—not lifeless. They were frozen and hard, but there was anger lurking in those dark depths, anger that swirled between them now like the dank fog rolling past the windows.

Terrifying eyes on a terrifying man. No wonder the former owners had been devastated when they'd finally lost control of Ashton House to this man. Poor Sara and Jonas. They'd tried valiantly to fend off the corporate raider, losing property after property to his insatiable greed.

Shock now turned to anger on their behalf. 'That's no reason for wanting to pull down such a beautiful building and destroy a thriving business in the process. What are the employees supposed to do?'

He shrugged, a careless hitch of his shoulders that ratcheted up her anger tenfold, before he sat up, turning his attention back to his breakfast. 'Find other jobs, I expect.'

'Just like that?'

'If they're any good, as they should be in a place that, as you say, claims to be the best, then it shouldn't be a problem.'

Every answer as callous as the one that went before. Every answer building on the burgeoning rage she already felt inside. But she'd be damned if he thought she was going to sit by and watch him destroy such a beautiful building—the very building in which her own parents had celebrated their marriage forty years ago—and jobs and careers into the deal. There had to be a way of saving the hotel from this madman. But she would need time.

'So when's all this supposed to happen?' she asked, doing all she could to keep the snarl out of her voice. 'Given we have forward bookings more than twelve months out, are you saying the hotel's got a year? Eighteen months? How much time will the staff have in order to find new positions elsewhere?'

He shook his head. 'No.'

'What do you mean, "no"?'

'I mean that there is hardly any point advising people that their positions will no longer be required in twelve months' time when they may well be gone in six. Then there would be positions to fill. Better that there is a clean break all around.'

'So...how long do we have?'

'The hotel will close in three months.'

'What? That's impossible. There's no way—'

'Ms Keogh, one thing I have learned in business is that nothing is impossible. The hotel will close. End of story.'

'But I...I can't let you do that.'

He laughed, and the sound fed into her anger.

'And how do you propose to stop me?'

'By convincing you that this property is worth much more to you as a going concern. I've prepared reports for you, projections—'

'You had a hearing,' he argued. 'You told me people come here for the view.' He lifted one hand towards the fog-laden exterior. 'So it's not like they'll be missing out on one hell of a lot if I close this place down, is it?'

Her knuckles turned white in her lap. 'It's winter in the Adelaide Hills, Mr Carrazzo. And, in winter, we sometimes get fog. Not every day. Not every other day. Just on occasion. This happens to be one such occasion.'

He didn't rush to respond, just bided his time that way he did, like he was bored and wanted to be done with it.

'Three months. That's all you have.'

Her anger turned incendiary. 'You're insane! You must be. What about all the forward bookings? We have weddings booked—and conferences. People have paid deposits. You can't just cancel them.'

'They will be cancelled. Compensated as well, if need be. As manager that will, of course, be your job.'

She scoffed. 'So you expect me to be the apologist for your act of bastardy? I don't think so.'

'You're refusing to do your job, Ms Keogh? I'm sure we could arrange an earlier termination for you if that's so. Say, today?'

Mackenzi gasped, the cold, hard reality that she might walk out of here jobless, not in three months but as soon as today, starting to bite. She was luckier than most—her home, a tiny stone cottage deeper in the hills, was almost paid off courtesy of a single life and a reasonable income. Still, a termination payment would keep her going only for how long?

On the other hand, there was definitely something to be said for getting out of here as soon as possible—very definitely before he discovered the truth. If she wasn't going to have a job in three months, that was one very attractive option.

'Put it like that,' she said, her voice crisp as frost as she made up her mind, 'and you leave me no choice. I'll go. Today.'

She had him there, she could see by the brief flicker of surprise across his features that her acceptance was the last thing he'd been expecting. He'd thought she was going to beg for her job—no way!

He raised one cynical eyebrow. 'Making the grand gesture? Don't expect me to ask you to stay on.'

It was liberating, she realized, losing your job. Empowering. For now there was no reason for her to curb her tongue; she no longer had a job to lose. And suddenly all the things she'd been itching to say since she'd first sat down could have their moment in the sun.

'You know, Mr Carrazzo,' she said with a smile, returning his own formality, 'despite what we'd heard, I actually believed there might be some point talking to you, some point in pleading our case to your better self. But there is no better self, is there? You really are a heartless bastard.'

'That's half my problem,' he acknowledged with his own wry smile, finding this intercourse much more enter-

taining than he'd been anticipating when the mouse had
first appeared. 'I do have a reputation to uphold.'

'I don't understand how you can sleep at night!'

'Is that why you provided the woman? Because you
assumed I'd need entertaining while my guilty conscience
kept sleep at bay?'

Twin slashes of red stained her cheeks. Her eyes shakily
held his before she hastily turned her face away, pretending an interest in the sea of fog beyond the glass, while in
her lap her hands twisted her napkin into a rope. 'I don't
know what you're talking about.'

Dante smiled at her. At least, he projected a smile, one
that would no doubt have made a crocodile proud. 'The
woman in my bed last night. You're the manager here.
Don't tell me you didn't arrange for her?'

Her eyes snapped back, her mouth set grimly, the
knotted napkin forgotten as she rose shakily to her feet. 'I
don't have to listen to this.'

He stood up and barred her exit from the table. 'Did you
honestly believe that having some whore waiting for me in
my bed last night was going to make me feel more kindly
towards keeping the hotel operating as a going concern?'

He watched her chin kick back on a swallow, saw her
hands fisting at her sides. 'So, tell me, where is this "whore"
now, Mr Carrazzo? Waiting for you to return for a repeat
performance of your no doubt magnificent services? I'm
surprised you could drag yourself out of bed.'

Her words grated, rubbing him raw. She knew more
than she was letting on, that was for sure, and she was
guilty as hell. They'd set him up with some whore in the
vain attempt that she might soften his intentions. Not likely,

especially when she'd barely managed to soothe anything before she'd so rapidly disappeared. 'You know she's gone. What were you doing—paying by the hour?'

'While I can quite understand why it would be necessary to pay anyone to sleep with you, Mr Carrazzo, I can assure you nobody was paid to be in your room. Maybe this so-called woman was never even there. Most likely she was just a figment of your imagination. So perhaps now you might let me pass? I have an office to clean out.'

His teeth ground together. Now she was laughing at him, her green eyes flashing like emeralds behind her modest glasses, the only splash of colour in her otherwise pale face.

Green eyes?

And suddenly he was back in his bed, her hair streaming across his pillow, the eyes he'd so wrongly imagined must be brown open wide in surprise.

Green eyes!

The same vivid green as those of the woman standing before him right now.

Mentally he unravelled the hair, now coiled tightly behind her head, peeled away the glasses and dispensed with her starched uniform—and every imaginary step only confirmed what his eyes had already told him to be true.

His hands found his hips while inside him anger rose like magma, his body tensing, a volcano about to erupt. Whatever game she was playing, it was game over. 'So tell me,' he invited, his teeth barely parting as he aimed the words like bullets, 'who is the better lover—me...' he paused for effect '...or Richard?'

CHAPTER FOUR

SHOCK MOMENTARILY punched the air from her lungs. She hadn't thought of Richard in days—no, more like weeks. At least, not until that dream last night, and then it had been only to wonder why he'd never made her feel as good as her dream lover.

But, just like her dream had never really been a dream at all, his question similarly had nothing to do with Richard.

He was telling her that she was the woman in his bed, the woman he'd called a whore.

He was telling her that he knew!

Fear pressed down on her, wrapping about her psyche like a cold, dank shroud.

'I…I've got no idea what you're talking about,' she lied, her mind furiously backtracking over her words, wondering what she'd done to give herself away, and wondering what she could do to make up for the gaffe.

'You mean Richard's never told you that you talk in your sleep?'

The waitress hovered nearby uncertainly, looking to make a move for his empty plate, and Mackenzi knew it was way past time to take this discussion out of a public restaurant and to somewhere much more private.

'If you've finished your breakfast, Mr Carrazzo, I think it's time we concluded this discussion in my office.'

'Alternatively, there's always my suite,' he suggested, cold civility in his tone and damnation in his eyes. 'You seemed to feel quite at home there last night.'

'That's enough!' she snapped, doing her best to ignore the shocked expression on the waitress's face, and the turning heads of curious patrons. She headed off purposefully through the tables on her way to the exit, leaving him to follow in her wake, half-hoping he wouldn't.

She'd taken his offer of redundancy thinking it would protect her identity. But now he knew she'd been the woman in his bed, the woman he'd decided to have sex with before she'd even been awake, the woman who had failed to turn him down even when she had finally opened her eyes.

Where did that leave her now?

'You didn't have to say those things,' Mackenzi asserted, rounding on him the moment he'd entered her office and closed the door behind him.

'And you didn't have to be in my bed.'

'I never said I was.'

'You didn't have to. Your reaction to the Richard word was confirmation enough.'

She looked away. 'That proves nothing. I was merely shocked at what you said.'

'Then why did you practically flee from the restaurant?'

'With you making accusations like that? Why do you think?'

'I think you're avoiding the truth.'

Dante paused, regarding her curiously for a few moments, before his hand went to the door once again, turning the key in the lock.

'What are you doing?' she protested, feeling a sudden surge of panic.

'You wanted privacy. I'm ensuring we get it.' Then he stepped closer, and all of a sudden she was regretting the move to her office. She'd wanted to get things less public, but suddenly the air in the room seemed to have been sucked out, the space shrinking to miniscule proportions now they were both locked inside it.

Shrinking until there was nothing in her office but Mackenzi Keogh and Dante Carrazzo, and the heavy weight of what had transpired between them in the early hours of the morning.

And the heavier weight of whatever was to come.

'So what did you really think you were going to achieve by pulling that little stunt last night?'

She backed away, trying to put the desk between them, but he only followed her, trapping her once again, her back to a filing cabinet in the space between desk and window. She crossed her arms defensively while he stood broad-shouldered in front of her. One arm was stretched across to the windowsill, the other hand planted on the desk, a human barricade. She had to hand it to him—this man made intimidation an art form. Even so, she was aware of the ever-present heat she felt in this man's presence steadily building up steam once again.

'I really don't see the point of continuing this line of conversation. Not when you've already decided on your course of action for the hotel and terminated my services. I'd rather you turned your mind to how you're going to inform the staff, and I'll get on with cleaning out my office.'

'Why not talk about it—because your little ploy didn't work?' His hand left the windowsill to reach out to her, stroking the line of her shirt's shoulder-seam. She flinched at his touch, his fingers scorching her flesh through her shirt, leaving a trail of fire in their wake. How was that possible? Sure, he'd made her feel good last night— amazing, in fact—but how could he still affect her when she hated the man? Because there was no way she couldn't hate him now with what he had planned for Ashton House.

Mackenzi stiffened her spine, determined not to let him see how his touch affected her, determined to deny everything. His assumption that everyone, including her, would be falling all over themselves to please him was enough to get her back up. 'What ploy?'

'To soften up my attitude. To make me feel more generous about the fate of the hotel. I must say, you do an impressive job of going above and beyond the call of duty.'

She shook her head as his hand moved down her arm, his thumb tracking perilously close to the swell of her breast. She could unfold her arms, but then she'd feel too exposed, too open to him, and he'd surely hear her heart thumping crazily. 'And *I* must say you have a very fertile imagination. Now, would you please leave me alone?'

'You didn't mind me touching you last night, as I recall. In fact, you seemed to enjoy it—a lot.'

She didn't want to hear it. Those feelings she'd experienced last night, the feelings she was having now when he merely brushed her arm or came close to her breasts, she didn't understand them. They were all too new, too unfamiliar. She didn't understand why this man, of all men, would be the one who would so comprehensively mess with her thermostat.

Frustrated, she unfolded her arms in a rush to fend him off as she tried to push past. 'You're mad. Let me out of here.'

But he just smiled and moved the same way so that their bodies collided. She bounced back from the contact, short of breath, only to have what breath was left in her throat wrenched away deftly as he removed her glasses, letting them fall gently onto the desk blotter beside them.

'Hey!'

His smile widened. 'You have the most amazing eyes,' he told her. 'They're the most brilliant shade of green—almost like emeralds. I knew I'd seen them somewhere before.'

She looked away. 'Lots of people have green eyes,' she said, only to feel his hand working at something behind her head. Before she could protest, she felt her hair slip free from its clasp, weight pulling it tumbling down over her shoulders and beyond, helped on its way with a comb of his fingers. Her scalp tingled, but it was her entire body that trembled. 'There, isn't that better?'

'Not really, no.'

He lifted a coil of her hair and snaked it around his fingers, dipping his head and inhaling deeply. 'I woke this morning with the scent of your hair on my pillow. Why did you leave so soon?'

'I still don't know what you're talking about.'

'You can't still pretend it wasn't you in my bed?'

'I told you, it was probably a dream.'

He tugged on her hair, drawing her closer. 'Oh, it was better than a dream. Much better.' His voice was a warm, silk ribbon that curled around her as his eyes held her prisoner. 'And so much more satisfying.'

He was too close. So close she could breathe in his own personal scent, between the shower freshness and breakfast coffee—a scent that flung her back, more than anything, to where she'd been just a few short hours ago. A scent that filled her lungs and was pumped around her bloodstream, reminding every last part of her of what they'd shared, and just how amazing he'd felt inside her. How he'd stretched her so deliciously. How he'd fitted her so completely.

She shook her head. She couldn't afford to think about that. 'Look, Mr Carrazzo—'

'Call me Dante.'

'Wh…?'

'After what happened last night, maybe it's time we were on first-name terms.'

Denial, she thought; there was still hope in denial. And in backing away. Even if there were only cold, hard filing cabinets at her back to welcome her. They were solid and real, and in a world where everything she knew had gone pear-shaped she needed their straight, metal lines and reassuring rigidity. '*Nothing* happened last night.'

He followed her, placing his hands on the cabinets either side of her. 'Why did you disappear? I missed you this morning.'

She was shaking her head. 'No.'

He lifted one hand to touch the pads of two fingers to her chin, tracing the line of her jaw to her ear, before letting his fingers trail down her neck. 'We had so much more to explore together.'

She dragged in a breath. 'I still say you're talking to the wrong person.'

His hand moved to her shoulder, cupping it in his warmth before trailing down her arm, his thumb venturing perilously close to the side of her breast. 'It seems such a shame to leave things like that—just when they were getting interesting.'

She tried and failed to shrug him off. 'Look, this has gone far enough. I have packing to do, and you have a hotel to dismantle.'

'Indeed. But right now I think there's something we'd both rather be doing.'

'No!'

He smiled then, a smile that did nothing to warm his coldly calculating eyes. Mackenzi shivered anew, feeling like some kind of prey about to be swallowed up whole, and all she knew was that she'd had enough.

'Because I know you enjoyed last night's sex,' he said. 'Just as much as I did.'

'I did not!' And the very moment she'd uttered the denial she wanted to take it back, wanted to delete it from history so she could keep on avoiding the truth, keep from seeing the flash of victory that had turned his dark eyes triumphant. She lifted a hand to her mouth, but it was too late to call back the words, too late to stop the keening cry of despair that followed them.

Could this day possibly get any worse?

'There there, Ms Keogh,' he said, placing both hands behind her neck, stroking her. 'You tried and you failed. Don't beat yourself up about it.'

His patronizing words were all she needed to feel some of her fight return. She might have nothing left to defend but she could still attack. She lifted her hands, putting away his arms. 'I cannot believe your arrogance. You find a woman asleep in a bed and you assume she's there for your own sexual gratification. What kind of man are you?'

'A man who doesn't look a gift welcome package in the mouth.'

'You make it sound like I was waiting for you.'

'Weren't you? You were right there in my suite. Naked in my bed. And the night clerk had filled me in on the fact the staff had arranged a little something for me. So considerate. My only regret is that the welcome package didn't hang around long enough for me to truly appreciate her. Why did you leave so abruptly, Ms Keogh? We'd hardly had a chance to get to know one another.'

Facts grated uncomfortably together like a bad gear-change in her head as the true horror of how the situation had arisen emerged. He thought she'd been part of some 'welcome package'? Had he even noticed the basket of local cheeses and wines that had been assembled for him and left waiting on the suite's coffee-table?

Clearly not. She swallowed. He'd accepted that the hotel was supplying him with a whore to earn his favour, and he'd assumed she was that whore. And she certainly hadn't helped her cause by not having let him know last night that his attentions weren't welcome.

Although they had been. She squeezed her eyes shut. She'd had the opportunity to leave if she'd wanted it. There had been plenty of time for her to flee his bed if she hadn't imagined her bones turned to jelly. And now how could she pretend she hadn't wanted him to make love to her when she'd been so actively involved?

How could she turn around and claim she hadn't been there for the very reason he'd alleged?

She had two choices: tell him he'd been wrong about the reason she'd been in his bed, admit she'd worked late and that the hotel had been full, and that because he hadn't been expected before breakfast she'd decided to steal nothing more than a few hours' precious sleep in the only vacant bed in the hotel—and make herself look as naïve and stupid as she felt.

Or bluff it out. Play him at his own game and pretend to accept that her so-called 'ploy' hadn't worked, and at least walk out of here with some miniscule piece of pride left intact.

It wasn't that difficult a decision to make.

'So what was the point of hanging around?' Mackenzi said, angling up her chin. 'It was all over in a minute, after which you promptly rolled over and went to sleep. Hardly worth hanging around for.'

The cockiness slid from his face, her insult finding its mark. '*All over in a minute?* Seems to me I remember you enjoying every second of that minute.'

She shrugged. 'It was okay, I guess.'

Dante's eyes narrowed, and she could see she'd just handed him the worst insult possible. 'And you didn't think you'd wait around and see what the morning brought?'

She shrugged. 'I'm sorry, but it seemed like such a ridiculous idea when I thought about it. You clearly agree. I mean, it's obvious you're not the type of man who'd change his mind about what he had planned for the hotel just because of one night in the sack.'

He wanted to growl. Not only was she happy to insult his manhood, but she was the only woman who had decided she'd had enough before he had. And he didn't like it one bit.

'And so you pretended to know nothing—to deny it had ever happened—even after I recognized you?'

She gave a jerky laugh, making a play of pushing back her hair with one hand. 'It's hardly the sort of thing you want to confess. I thought it better to deny all knowledge and write it off to experience.'

'And what if there was more than one night?'

She hesitated. 'I don't follow you.'

'You said I'd never change my mind about the hotel because of one night in the sack. You're right. But what if you had longer? Could you change my mind, do you think?'

Her eyes narrowed, her head already moving into a shake. 'I need to clear out this office. I don't have time for this.'

'Then make time. You might learn something. It might interest you to know that most people fail in achieving their goals because they quit too early.'

'Look, thanks for the life lesson, but you really should be going if you're going to make that ten-thirty meeting to tell the staff you're about to knock the hotel out from under their feet, and if I'm going to have a hope of getting this office packed up.'

'I'm serious,' he said.

She paused. 'About what?'

'About wanting to sleep with you again.'

Somewhere down the hall a phone rang. A cleaning trolley rattled past, and beyond the windows the impenetrable fog continued to swirl.

'That's not funny,' she said, her voice sounding tight and strained.

'I'm not laughing.'

And he wasn't, not the way his jaw was set, his dark eyes intent—intent on getting her back into his bed. A tremor rolled through her at the possibility. The way he'd made her feel…

She grabbed a lungful of air. 'I don't want to sleep with you.'

'You already have.'

'It was a mistake. It shouldn't have happened. It won't again.'

'Not even if I change my mind?'

She didn't trust him as far as she could throw him, but neither could she ignore the slightest possibility he might change his mind. 'What do you mean?'

'You seem like the sort of person who would do almost anything to save your precious hotel.'

'I don't want Ashton House to close. Nobody does apart from you.'

'Then I'm giving you a chance to save it.'

'By sleeping with you? I don't believe you.'

His dark eyes gleamed. 'Believe it. Don't sleep with me, and the hotel will be closed down. Destroyed. Alternatively, sleep with me and you could single-handedly save it.'

She blinked. 'You're expecting me to become your mistress?'

He shrugged, as if it was little more than asking her to work through a lunch hour. 'Only for as long as it takes.'

'And, if I do, you'll agree not to close the hotel?'

'No. I'll agree to think about it.'

'You'll *think about it*? What kind of a deal is that?'

'The best deal you're going to get today.'

'And what's to say you have any intention of *thinking about it* at all? How do I know you won't carry out your plans to close the hotel anyway?'

'You don't.'

Mackenzi shook her head. 'You really are insane.' She grabbed a box of paper, taking out the remaining reams before tossing items from her desk into it.

She reached for a photo but his hand stayed her, his fingers circling her wrist before she could grasp it. She looked down on it with disdain. 'You might fancy yourself as a top-notch businessman, but you've got one hell of a lot to learn about romance.'

He didn't let go. 'Think about it,' he said. 'Do you really want to front your associates in a few minutes and tell them that you'd been offered a chance to save the hotel, and maybe their jobs, but you'd turned the opportunity down flat?'

'It won't be me fronting that meeting. You've already made me redundant, remember?'

'Then I'll tell them.'

She looked up at him in shock, unable to believe even he could be that cruel.

'I'll tell them that since I didn't have the co-operation of the manager I had no choice but to make a decision to close it down.'

'You wouldn't dare.'

He smiled. 'Try me.'

It was insane. He couldn't mean it. She thought of the staff—of Natalie on Reception, who'd just bought her first home, of the chef, Con, whose wife was expecting their third child. Could she do it to them—deny them the one chance they might have to keep their jobs longer than three months?

It was wrong, so wrong, and yet the thought of making love to him again…and the knowledge that he wanted to make love to her…

The ancient clock on the mantelpiece chimed out the half-hour, and she looked over at it in panic.

'It's announcement time,' he said, edging closer, touching the pads of his fingers to her cheek, trailing them down her neck, his touch electric. 'So what's it to be? Close down the hotel, or warm my bed and give your colleagues a fighting chance? It's up to you.'

Mackenzi shied away from his hand, more to hide the tremors that resonated through her than from any revulsion at his touch. 'With no guarantees, of course?'

'Life doesn't come with guarantees. Yet we still have to make decisions every day. This is just one more. The fate of Ashton House is up to you. Decide.'

She squeezed her eyes shut, wishing she could so easily block out the scent of him, and the acute awareness of his presence that fired her skin to simmering heat.

It was an outrageous demand, no kind of deal at all, and she should turn him down flat. But in standing up for herself she'd be letting the hotel down. And in agreeing to share his bed there would be just the glimmer of a chance that the hotel might be spared after all.

Did she really have a choice?

'Yes,' she whispered through lips suddenly ash-dry, while other parts of her body warmed and bloomed in certain knowledge of what was to come.

'I didn't hear you,' he said, extracting every last shred of humiliation from her.

'Yes,' she repeated, louder this time. 'I'll sleep with you.'

Dante smiled then, a smile that simultaneously turned her thoughts to panic, and her nipples to bullets. 'I knew you'd see reason.'

Was it reason she'd seen? As he came closer, all reason seemed to turn tail and flee, the fire ignited in his eyes melting any remaining hint of resistance. Fear mingled with anticipation as he stood before her. Was this the real reason he'd locked the door behind him? Surely he wouldn't demand she commence her duties so soon?

'We have a meeting—'

'Turn around,' he ordered.

'What?'

'Turn around!'

She dragged in air, needing oxygen desperately, but finding it infused with the rich pull of his scent, the rich heat of him, as she turned shakily towards the desk.

'What are you doing?' she asked, but all too soon his purpose was patently clear as she felt her skirt being hitched up from behind, his hands scorching a trail up her thighs. She gasped and pushed herself closer to the desk, anything to increase the distance between them, but he only followed her, his fingers curling around her legs, pulling her back towards him at the same time he pressed himself close up behind her.

He laughed, a rough sound, like he was battling with himself. 'You see how much I want you?'

She gasped, as through the bunched-up fabric of her skirt she could feel his hard length. Through the throbbing at the apex of her thighs she could feel her own need. Her own wants. But it was too soon, her agreement too raw, his needs too powerful.

'Stop it,' she pleaded. Meaning it. Not meaning it. 'Please…'

His mouth took to her neck, moving over her in a liquid motion of pleasure, his body spooned behind hers as if they were almost one. *As surely they soon would be.*

'You want this,' he uttered, his lips and breath dancing over sensitive skin. 'You want me.'

'Not like this,' she protested, even as her body bloomed with a desire so thick and languid it threatened to buckle her knees. *And certainly not yet.* 'I said I would share your bed, not be taken like some Neanderthal's woman.'

CHAPTER FIVE

DANTE'S MOUTH stilled and lifted from her throat, the exploration of his hungry hands arrested. 'What did you call me?'

In the momentary respite, Mackenzi found reserves she'd never known she had and spun herself away, dragging her skirt back down to her knees in the process. 'What do you expect? Your caveman tactics may have got you to where you are in business, but you can leave them behind when it comes to the bedroom.'

His nostrils flared, and his hands balled into fists at his hips. 'Have you forgotten,' he uttered through teeth tightly clenched, 'that it was you who turned up naked in my bed? And it was you who agreed to become my mistress? And now you think you have a choice?'

She tossed him a throwaway shrug, the merest concession to the truth of his assertion. Because she *had* agreed to become his mistress, and she was as good as his—lock, stock and barrel. 'I never agreed I'd like it.'

His eyes gleamed dangerously, as if she'd just issued him with some kind of challenge. 'I promise you, if enjoyment is what you're after, you'll get it.' Once again he moved closer, with his wild-looking eyes, and his breathing building, every bit as ragged as her own, when a knock at the door halted his progress.

'Miss Keogh?' the hesitant voice called uncertainly, the handle turning fruitlessly as their visitor found the door locked. 'The meeting… The staff are waiting.'

Dante still held her eyes prisoner, and yet for the first time she felt like she'd won some kind of battle against this man—if only a battle to gain some time. She turned on a smile designed to reflect her small victory as she called out, 'We'll be right there.'

How she made it through the meeting, she didn't know. Especially when Dante announced that Mackenzi would be stepping down from her direct-managerial position and be 'assisting' him with his deliberations while he assessed the credentials of the hotel. Every pair of eyes suddenly turned her way.

What must they all be thinking? There would be talk, she had no doubt—from the waitress at breakfast who'd heard his dig about her being in his suite, to the clerk who must have been wondering why voices were raised and her office door locked, from everyone here questioning her less-than-immaculate hair that she'd twisted and shoved a clip into before heading for this meeting. She could see the questions in their eyes. She could feel the heat of her own self-damning response as colour flooded her cheeks.

But then he announced that until a decision was made it would be business as usual, and she'd seen their attention turn back to him and their curiosity turn to relief. The relief that the axe they'd been expecting hadn't yet fallen, and that their jobs were safe, at least for now. She was almost happy that she'd made the decision she had.

Almost.

Until someone asked how long the process would take, and Dante tossed off a careless, 'A week, maybe two,' bringing home how little hope she had of changing his mind, bringing home how little she was worth. Two weeks at the most to make him realize the value of Ashton House before he discarded her. Two weeks where he would use her, peel her like an orange, devour her and spit out the pips.

He glanced at her then, his eyes like deep, dark pools of promise, and she shuddered at what she saw there: desire. Need. Hunger.

Her body responded in kind, her breasts firming, the fire in her belly sending flames licking dangerously lower, building an inexorable head of steam inside her.

How long would he wait to take her again? He'd already shown he was a man with a powerful appetite for sex. She'd thwarted him once by escaping from his room while he'd slept. She'd evaded him the second time by insulting him and halting him in his carnal tracks. But how long could she avoid the inevitable? How long could she hold him at bay?

How long did she really *want* to?

One week, maybe two, was all he'd estimated she'd last. After the sexual awakening she'd had last night, the extraordinary feelings unleashed within her, somehow one to two weeks didn't seem anywhere near enough.

'Pack your things,' he told her once the last question had been answered and the staff had dispersed and returned to their duties, relieved that they still for now had duties to return to.

'Excuse me?'

'We're leaving. After lunch.'

'But you didn't say anything about—'

'I have a business to run. I need to be where my business takes me.'

While you can be my mistress anywhere.

The unspoken words hung in the space between them, as cold and hard as a slap in the face. If he'd wanted to make their respective positions more clear, he couldn't have done a better job. But she'd agreed to this. He'd typecast her as a whore, and so far, even if reluctantly, she was living up to his expectations.

'So where are we going?'

'First to Melbourne. Then onto Auckland. I have a deal to close. It can't wait any longer.'

If he was trying to impress her with his hectic schedule, it wasn't working. 'I suppose we should be flattered you took the time to come here at all.'

He looked at her levelly, the eyes that just a few minutes ago had set fire to her blood now glacial cruel, and laced with rapier-sharp pain that was almost tangible. 'This was personal.' Then he blinked, and when he reopened his eyes whatever she'd seen there had gone. She might even have thought she'd imagined it, if she hadn't still felt the effect of that cold, unseeing stare at her very core.

He pulled a card from his wallet. 'Call my PA. She needs your details.' He hesitated. 'You have got a passport?'

She allowed herself a smile, almost wishing she hadn't. Wouldn't that put a spanner in his works? But it would also put a spanner in hers. No matter what she thought of him, the hotel would have no chance at all if she couldn't fulfil her end of the bargain. And, for her own selfish reasons, this was one bargain she was determined to fulfil. But be damned if she was going to roll over with her legs in the air—even if that was what he expected. 'It would be a bit hard to trail after you as your mistress otherwise.'

His eyes chilled once again. 'You wanted a lifeline for your precious hotel. You got it. So don't make out you don't get anything out of this. We leave at two. Be ready.'

He turned to go, a man on a mission, leaving her shaking in his wake.

'Do I have a choice?' she called after him.

He looked back over his shoulder at her. 'No.'

The fog was starting to lift as she pulled her ancient car into her even more ancient driveway, tiny patches of blue colouring the sky in places. Ahead of her emerged the misty outline of the old stone house. She pulled up in the old stables that now served as a garage and checked her watch. It had been a slow trip home, but she had just enough time to ask Mrs Gepp next door if she could feed Misty for the next however-long, dust off her passport, call her parents and get some clothes together.

She dropped her head down onto the steering wheel, suddenly realising what she was doing. Now the adrenaline was gone and shock was setting in. In the space of the last twenty-four hours she'd managed to have mind-blowing sex with the boss, discover her beloved hotel was about to be destroyed, lose her job, and promptly become her boss's mistress. Just another day at the office.

Oh God, what was happening to her?

Running on empty, feeling heartsick, she forced herself

from the car even though the thought of firing up the ignition and heading somewhere else—anywhere else— seemed far more attractive. She'd agreed to this, so how could she get out of it now? And how could she walk away from the hotel's one chance of survival? She knew she only had a slim chance, if that, but knowing Dante if she ran now he'd probably close the hotel tomorrow.

So she had to focus. She had to deal with it. Even calling on the memories of great sex, unexpectedly great sex that had told her she wasn't as cold as she'd feared—great sex she wouldn't mind engaging in again—even with those memories and needs she knew she must have been insane to agree to this.

So instead she shoved her doubts aside, and tried to focus on her list. Lists she could deal with. Lists she could tackle.

Getting the cat organized was the easiest.

The phone call to her parents was the hardest. How to avoid informing her parents of the fact you'd been made redundant today, and yet were going away 'on business', was harder than she'd imagined. She hated lying to her parents, even by omission, but there were some things that shouldn't be shared.

Especially when they asked about the hotel and whether she had any idea what the new owner had planned for it. She'd known they would ask, and she squeezed her eyes shut. Her parents had been married at Ashton House. They had happy memories, spending each and every anniversary in the restaurant, reliving old memories with their friends. 'It's still up in the air,' she told them in all honesty. 'Maybe soon we'll have good news.' And she crossed her fingers and hoped that was true.

Half an hour later she'd accomplished the first three items on her list and was staring into her open wardrobe doors contemplating the last, Misty doing lazy figure-eights around her ankles and purring as if she didn't have a care in the world.

Unlike Mackenzi.

'So, what do mistresses wear?' she asked her feline friend, but Misty just rolled onto her back and wriggled. Mackenzi sighed. Whatever they wore, she was sure the paltry contents of her closet were hardly going to make the grade.

She rifled past her spare uniforms, wrote off the shirts and casual trousers she reserved for days off working around her property, and located her couple of pairs of good trousers. One of them would do for travelling. She was just selecting a handful of tops to go with them when she found it: her one concession to glamour. The little beaded-black dress sat pristine in its dry-cleaning bag where it had been since its last outing a couple of years ago. The jet beads winked at her from the depths of her wardrobe. It could do with a run around the park.

She added it to the small pile on her bed, pushing Misty, who'd decided that the action was all happening on the bed, to one side in the process before locating shoes, underwear and accessories. Then, in a spike of perverse logic, she packed her thickest flannelette pyjamas. She still wasn't sure about this whole 'sex' thing. The memories from last night were still too raw and unprocessed in any logical way—at least flannelette would be reassuring until that happened.

Finally she changed out of her uniform into black trousers and a soft knitted top and stashed the rest of her things in a small suitcase. Her mistress wardrobe, such as it was. It would have to do.

There was the crunch of tyres along the driveway, followed by a spray of gravel, as whoever it was came to a sudden halt.

Misty looked up at her enquiringly from her place on the bed and blinked one eye. 'Don't ask me,' she told the cat as a car door slammed shut. But the way her heart had lurched told her it was him, even before anyone started pounding on her front door, even before she made it down the passageway and pulled open the solid-timber door, to find six-foot-four of barely concealed rage disguised as a man.

Yet even having sensed bone-deep that it was him didn't lessen the impact of seeing him in the flesh. He was so large, his stance so physically domineering, with his hands on hips and his eyes so wild, that it took her breath away.

He scowled. 'They said you'd gone.' It was an accusation.

Mackenzi regarded him with as much disdain as she could muster, and still it wasn't enough to help her meet his gaze and bear the impossible weight of those damning eyes. And, worse, it was nowhere enough to ignore the sexual pull of this man. Her senses drank him in like a drug, her memories coiled around her like a promise. *Damn him!*

'And so I had,' she fired back in exasperation. 'What of it?' She wheeled away from the door, heading for the kitchen. Heading anywhere that might take her away from this man.

Misty met her there, curling against her calves once more as she reached into the pantry for a can of cat food. She dipped one hand to pet the cat, and then turned to find him standing behind her, a wall of man. Her heart was hammering so loudly it was no wonder she hadn't heard him follow her, but finding him so close now sent her pulse into orbit.

'I tried to call you. Your phone was off.' Another accusation. What the hell was his problem?

She shook her head, as neatly she sidestepped around both him and the island bench, trying to think calmly. She had a man, a virtual stranger, in her kitchen—a powerful man with some kind of grudge against the whole world in general, and right now against her in particular. Why was he so angry with her? Because they'd had sex? Well, she wasn't crazy about the idea either. The sex had been good, but the source definitely left something to be desired.

She took a deep breath and pulled out the cutlery drawer, giving a wistful look at the knives before picking up a spoon. 'I didn't. It's just—'

'I tried to call. Your phone was off!'

She popped the ring pull and ripped off the lid, metal scraping open, the sound mirroring her grating nerves, before the smell of sardines and tuna assailed her nostrils, threatening her churning stomach. 'My phone *is* on. It's just the hills, they sometimes block the signal.'

'You're lying.'

'And you're insane. You show up here like Rambo, all guns blazing, and for what? Did you think I was trying to run away or something?'

'Were you?'

She scoffed. 'I wish. And do you think anyone would blame me? But no, we had a deal, remember? *I* do, even if it was a deal I was blackmailed into.' She tossed the lid into the sink for now and plunged the spoon into the silver-and-pink mixture.

'A deal,' he said, 'that you agreed to.'

He was standing between her and Misty's bowl, so she circled to the left, keeping the timber island between them.

She crouched down low, spooning the seafood into the bowl. Misty stood guard until she'd finished, glaring at their unwelcome visitor, her tail pointing directly into the air, until Mackenzi stood up and Misty relaxed enough to gobble down her food.

So he'd found her gone, hadn't been able to raise her on her mobile and had decided she'd changed her mind. 'You really thought I'd done a runner, didn't you? So, true to form, you had to do the caveman thing and come drag me back to your cave again. How sweet. I didn't realize you cared.'

Fury, white-hot and bitter, surged through his veins. Yes, he'd been angry when he'd discovered her missing from the hotel—especially when he'd discovered how far away she lived. He hadn't been overly worried that she'd reneged on their deal and run away, though. She needed this deal more than he did. But, when he hadn't been able to reach her on her mobile, the doubts had crept in.

She tossed the tin in the rubbish bin and moved back towards the sink, and he surprised her by moving in her path, his large hands hot around her arms. The spoon dropped unheeded from her hand, clattering on the terracotta-tiled floor. 'You want to see a caveman? I could take you right now,' he said. 'I could bend you over this damned bench you keep hiding behind and finish what I started before.'

Her eyes widened, her breath hitching up a notch telling him that it was more than shock that prompted her reactions. Her face was flushed, her breasts strained against the knit top and her nipples budded oh, so temptingly—but it was her eyes that gave her away, green eyes that flared with passion and barely repressed sexual need. Oh yes, she wanted this too.

The pink tip of her tongue emerged, moistening her top lip, and he watched it, fascinated. 'And wouldn't that just prove my point?' she said, her voice shaky and a little breathless.

Dante stepped her back until the island bench stopped her, then placed his hands beside her, imprisoning her in the space between his arms. 'Right now,' he whispered, his voice low and gravelly, 'I don't give a damn about your point. Because right now…'

He saw a moment's panic in those green depths, but it was just as quickly swallowed up in the flames that followed it. Flames of desire. For all her bluster, for all her 'caveman' rhetoric, she couldn't wait to start work as his mistress, in his bed or out of it. Even now he could sense her will buckling as her body prepared to make him welcome. Already she would be wet and slick and hot for him. He smiled and dipped his head lower, liking the way she angled her head in readiness for his kiss, her lips slightly parting. She probably didn't even realize she was doing it.

'Right now,' he repeated, his lips hovering bare millimetres from hers, 'we have a plane to catch.'

Mackenzi blinked, confusion warring with a certain disappointment in her eyes as he pushed himself away. 'Have you packed?'

She battled to gather herself, making a play of picking up the spoon and wiping at the floor where it had landed, keeping her face averted even though it was too late for that. He'd already seen the twin slashes of red that branded her cheeks. 'Of course I've packed,' she told him, in a voice that was a shadow of its former argumentative self. 'But you said we didn't have to leave until two.'

'Change of plans. We're flying out of Adelaide now, not driving, and going straight through to Auckland tonight. That's why I was trying to call you. Are you ready? Said all your goodbyes?'

She sniffed, ignoring his questions. 'I'll get my bag.'

'So you live alone?' Dante asked her halfway during the short flight to Melbourne.

They were the first words he'd spoken to her for what seemed like forever; his laptop and papers were spread out all around him, keeping him fully focused until now. She preferred it when he was fully focused on his work. It was easier to pretend that she was cool about this whole mistress thing, easier to pretend that it was just another day in the office.

She put down her novel, thankful that the wide business-class seats at least afforded her a degree of separation from him that she wouldn't have had in economy class. Not that she could imagine Dante slumming it in cattle class. He'd have trouble folding his long body into the constraints of one of those seats, for a start.

'You were there at the house,' she said at last. 'Did you see anyone else?' He'd followed her into her room when she'd retrieved her case—he'd raised an eyebrow at the size, or lack of it. And she hadn't missed his eagle-eyed appraisal of her house, taking it all in, searching for something—evidence of cohabitation? 'It's just me and Misty.'

'So who's Richard?'

Oh God, they were back to this. But then Dante Carrazzo didn't strike her as the kind of man who'd like to share. 'Nobody. A man I knew once. A friend.'

'A lover?'

She almost laughed. Richard had fancied himself as a lover, that was true, even if she'd never lived up to his expectations. Then she remembered the too-easy smiles, the too-easy charm—the too-easy hurt—and she frowned instead. 'For a time, I guess you could say that.'

'What happened?'

'He lied to me. Simple as that. He lied to me about something important and I could never trust him again.'

'What did he lie about?'

This time she did allow herself a laugh, a self-deprecating laugh, bitter and short. 'He was married. The whole time he was with me, he had a wife and two kids tucked away in Sydney. Little surprise he went away on business a lot. He obviously told his wife the same thing.'

He said nothing for a while, and she was beginning to think she'd bored him rigid with her pathetic recollection.

'You thought I was Richard last night.'

'Did I? I can't imagine why.' And that, at least, was the truth. Richard had been an adequate lover; he'd certainly thought so. He'd gone through the mechanics of sex with a textbook precision she had no doubt he employed in every facet of his MBA life. But, for all his charm, good looks and easy smiles, he'd failed to get her pulse racing, just as he'd never once blown her world apart.

She was an ice queen, he'd told her. He loved her, he'd told her—another lie—but she had a fundamental problem and she was lucky she had him to help her through it.

Coming after a first ill-fated romance, she had started to believe he was right.

Until last night, when Dante had blown her away, and kept threatening to do again every time they were alone together.

What was it about this man with dark, turmoil-filled eyes, who bullied and forced her into a deal she had no idea he'd even honour? A man who taunted her unmercifully, who threatened her with sex on a kitchen bench-top and then deprived her of the same.

Cheated her of the same.

Surely she should hate a man like that?

It was a kind of hate, she told herself. A simmering resentment for all that he had done and all that he had assumed. The scene in the kitchen played over again—the anticipation, the sheer depths of disappointment when she'd all but offered herself to him and he'd walked away. Oh yes, a blistering resentment for all that he *hadn't* done.

Less than twenty-four hours after one chance bedroom encounter, one bedroom awakening, and her body was practically begging for more of the same. She couldn't even kid herself she was only interested in sleeping with him for the lifeline it gave the hotel. Not any more.

Damn the man; she'd take the lifeline, but she also wanted what he could offer her.

And she wanted it bad.

The pilot's voice sounded over the intercom, informing them that they'd started their descent into Melbourne. The first leg of their journey was nearly over. Dante packed away his laptop and returned to his reports, saving her from any more questions but unable to save her from her thoughts.

Dante's investment manager, Adrian Stokes, met them

at the airport. A tall, pigeon-chested man with sandy, receding hair, he gave her a curious once-over like she was no more than some shell someone had collected on a beach. And then he proceeded to ignore her. Which suited her just fine. The two men obviously wanted to discuss business, so it was an easy decision to swap seats so the two of them could spend the entire next leg to New Zealand plotting whatever corporate uber-plan it was they were hatching.

It was easier sitting apart, her headphones delivering a constant supply of her favourite country-ballads over the drone of the engines. She stole a glance across the aisle, saw their heads bowed together in fervent conversation, Dante's long fingers wrapped around a fountain pen, his expression serious. It was easier, and she knew she should feel relieved. Yet part of her missed that almost electric sensation that accompanied his proximity, part of her missed the energy he radiated, the sizzle on her skin when they touched, the *danger*.

If she'd ever wondered what it meant to be a mistress, now she knew—having had his attention to herself for almost an entire day, only then to find herself being shoved aside to make way for his business associate, someone who could help him build his fortune to even greater heights. She was an indulgence. A diversion. Merely one or two weeks of down-time entertainment for a busy empire-builder.

The same one or two weeks she had to convince him not to close down Ashton House.

She'd been a fool today, pushing him away, insulting him at every opportunity and testing his limits, thinking this was all about her. It wasn't, not in the wider sense. She was just the vehicle. Because it was about saving Ashton House, and if she couldn't win this man over in bed how could she ever expect him to relent about the fate of the hotel?

Damn it all, she might only be his mistress, but that didn't mean she was without influence.

One or two weeks of opportunity.

And she wouldn't waste another minute of it. Starting right now.

She turned her head, caught his eye this time, held it, and smiled.

He was halfway through outlining their strategy for tomorrow's meeting with Quinn when he saw her. He paused, confused when for once she didn't look away and bury her face in her book. Confused even more when she smiled. What was that about?

'Dante?'

He looked back at Adrian, who was staring at him, frowning. 'You were saying?'

'Of course,' he said. 'Where was I?'

'She's kind of pretty,' Adrian conceded, throwing a glance Mackenzi's way, and clearly ready for a change of topic. 'Even though she could do with a nose job.'

Dante frowned. He didn't think her nose was that bad. Kind of cute, in a way.

'Her name sounds familiar,' Adrian added.

'It should. She's the ex-manager of Ashton House.'

Adrian's eyebrows shot up. 'Ah, she's a woman.'

'Very much so.'

Adrian grinned. 'And so she agreed to come along for the ride, given she was going to lose her job when you shut the hotel anyway?'

'Not quite. Mackenzi was quite vocal in her objections

to me closing down the hotel. I made a deal with her—if she'd come with me, I'd think about changing my mind.'

Adrian's smile widened, his eyes glinting as if he'd been let in on a delicious secret. 'You told her you'd *think* about it?'

It was Dante's turn to smile. 'That's about the size of it.'

'But you're not going to change your mind about Ashton House, are you? That's never going to happen.'

Dante took one last glance at Mackenzi, now engrossed again in her novel. He could almost feel sorry for her— almost. Then he turned his attention back to the figures. 'Not a chance.'

It was one in the morning by the time they landed in Auckland, closer to two by the time they'd disembarked and cleared customs, and another hour more by the time the stretch limousine had deposited them all at their hotel and they'd checked in. With the time difference, it was really closer to her midnight, but after a broken night's sleep last night, and a day fraught with tension today, Mackenzi's sleep-deprived body could easily have accepted the time as a fact. In any one else's presence.

Even Adrian's non-stop tale of matters at 'Carrazzo central'—his pet name for the Melbourne head office— during the ride into the sleeping city hadn't dulled her senses. In fact it had only sharpened her resentment of the man, as he'd pointedly ignored her throughout. She wondered if Adrian was an MBA. She didn't like him already.

Then Adrian was gone, and there was something about being led through the hushed hallways of a sleeping hotel, being led to *their* suite—the suite in which she would properly become his mistress—which made nonsense of the hour and honed her senses to wide-eyed wakefulness.

Would Dante expect her to commence her duties tonight, having found her a bed like she'd demanded? After experiencing his sensual tug on her most of the day, a tug that had threatened to bring her undone at least twice, she didn't doubt it.

The porter ushered them into their suite, but instead of the bed she'd been expecting to confront there was a lounge, large and plush and rich with sateens and velvet upholstery. A dining room for eight adjoined it, the table set with a massive floral centrepiece. A room to one side served as an office. At the far side of the suite lay the master bedroom—the size of a generous suite itself. The super king-sized bed piled with pillows dominated the spacious room, a tray on the table alongside bearing an ice bucket with a bottle of champagne and two crystal flutes.

But it was the bed her eyes returned to.

She gulped. A person could get lost in a bed that big. Then she looked at Dante, directing the porter with their bags, and changed her mind. She'd never be lost with him alongside. She trembled at the prospect. What would it be like to share his bed? To go to bed with him at night and wake up to him in the morning? How would it feel to have his body nestled against her own?

Soon she would find out.

She crossed to the large bank of windows and opened the net curtains, revealing the lights of the city in all their glory. Dante saw the porter out. She heard the door to their suite and finally, once again, they were alone.

At last!

CHAPTER SIX

ANTICIPATION curled and danced in her gut and she trembled anew, wrapping her hands around her midriff and clutching hold of her arms. She heard his approaching footfall on the plush carpet, and knew exactly the moment when he entered the room—but she refused to turn or acknowledge him, lest her features give too much away.

'Do you want anything from room service?'

She shook her head. 'No,' she said, her voice little more than a croak.

She heard him moving around behind her, unzipping his case, rattling in the closet. 'Then just make yourself at home. I shouldn't be too long.'

This time she turned around. 'Too long?'

There was a knock on the door. 'That'll be Adrian and the finance people,' he said, picking up his briefcase.

'It's three o'clock in the morning!'

'We'll be in the office. We'll try not to disturb you.' And he pulled the bedroom door closed behind him.

Mackenzi stood there, staring disbelievingly at the window. What kind of people held business meetings at three in the morning? She heard their low, muffled voices as they entered the suite and she felt the suite go quiet as they were ushered into the office and the solid door closed between them. She felt the ease with which he'd abandoned her like a slap in the face.

She paced the room for what seemed like forever, and skimmed her way through a dozen pointless television channels before deciding that, if she couldn't beat him, she might as well avoid him. With a grateful sigh of thanks for her foresight, she donned her flannelette pyjamas and slipped between the covers, lying in the endless wide bed in the dark with only the lights of the city for company. She wasn't waiting up for him, she told herself, she wasn't disappointed. So why did she feel frustrated beyond belief?

The glare of a brand new morning through uncovered windows woke her. That and the sound of the shower as she came to in a dizzy panic, wondering where she was, instantly remembering, and cursing herself for falling asleep. How could she not have noticed Dante coming to bed? He'd proven the night before that he made no concessions to a sleeping woman.

She looked around, but the other pillows lay where she'd left them, still in pristine condition, untouched, the rest of the expanse of bed-covers smooth.

He hadn't come to bed.

He emerged from the bathroom a few moments later, padding across to the closet, a towel at his waist the only attempt at modesty. The dizzy sense of detachment she'd had on wakening returned tenfold. His hair was finger-combed and still damp, his face rugged and unshaven and muscles packed his skin, sculpting his flesh into an artist's delight. A *woman's* delight.

And yet he wasn't handsome, not in a classic way. He was chiselled and rugged and solid as rock. In a suit he looked potent enough. Near naked, freshly showered, he looked positively dangerous. She wanted to experience that danger again. She wanted to feel his power unleashed inside her.

Under the flannelette of her pyjamas her skin grew prickly and tight, her breasts heavy and instantly peaking. Did he have any idea how much she wanted him right now? Would it make a difference if he did?

She shifted herself up against her pillows, letting the covers slide down enough to reveal the low V of her top. He looked her way, captured her appraisal and held it, his eyes looking her over, as cold and assessing as calculator buttons as he reached into the closet. 'Good morning. Sleep well?'

She had in the end. Surprisingly well. But that didn't make up at all for her feelings of abandonment and her resentment of the same. 'Better than you, I imagine.'

'We pulled an all-nighter. There's a problem with the zoning. Adrian thinks we've got it covered.'

He casually unhitched the towel, letting it fall at his feet and scrambling her brain in the process. He was half-erect, already magnificent, and her mouth went dry as every bit of moisture headed south. 'What are you planning on doing today?'

She turned herself sideways, damning her decision to wear pyjamas at all, but knowing very well how her unfettered décolletage would look at this angle.

Whatever you're planning, she wanted to say, *I'm ready.*

But she couldn't. She wanted him to come to her. She wanted him to think it was his idea. She wasn't about to beg.

With little more than a glance in her direction he pulled on a pair of black-silk underpants and resentment piled up anew, quashing all hope that this simmering need would be sated any time soon. He had to be kidding! How was she supposed to be his mistress if he wouldn't even come to bed?

'How long will you be?'

'As long as it takes,' he said grimly, donning a fresh shirt and tie. 'Why don't you go shopping? You didn't bring many clothes. You can charge anything in the boutique downstairs to the room.'

The doorbell rang as he put the finishing touches to his suit, and he left to open the door, coming back sipping on a coffee.

'I ordered breakfast,' he told her as he checked the contents of his briefcase and snapped it closed. 'Coffee, croissants and cooked breakfast. Okay?'

No sex on toast? Not okay at all. 'You're not eating, then?'

'I'll get something at the meeting.' He checked his watch. 'Anything you need, just call room service.'

She nodded dumbly, knowing room service didn't have what she wanted on the menu, wondering if she should tell him.

But damn him to hell and back. She wouldn't beg. She still had some pride left. Not much, admittedly, given the way she was feeling right now, but some.

The day was not going well. The zoning regulations that Adrian had assured him were under control were a complete and utter balls-up, and Quinn was playing hardball, thinking he'd found a flaw in their attack. Which he had.

The boardroom was stuffy as he listened to Adrian battle to claw back the ground he'd lost, the table surrounded by too many non-players that Quinn had dragged in to bolster his numbers. Dante was becoming more and more impatient as the deal that had looked in the bag was in danger of going belly-up. Something would have to give, but it sure as hell wouldn't be him.

But unless he could find a way to apply the screws he was less and less sure of his ground.

Alongside the crusty shell at the opposite end of the table that was Quinn, sat his PA, feverishly minuting everything that was said. She was too young, too frenetic; he hadn't given the ruddy-cheeked girl a second glance until she'd paused to jam her glasses higher up her nose and he'd noticed: green-lined eyelids, emphasizing eyes that were less than startling in colour. Mackenzi didn't need that stuff, he decided, thinking back, remembering the emerald-green eyes he'd been forced to leave smouldering in bed this morning.

Despite the unexpected flannelette pyjamas, he'd been aroused the minute he'd seen her still lying asleep in bed, her rich reddish-brown hair swathed across her pillow, her bold features at rest. And then he remembered the way she'd looked when she'd awoken, her eyes still slumberous and seductive, and the way she'd leaned sideways, exposing her creamy, honeyed cleavage to his gaze.

Not nearly enough of it for his liking.

Even though at the time his thoughts had been filled with the complexities of the day to come, walking away had been one of the hardest things he'd ever done. For a heartbeat he'd been tempted to join her, even if the team had been waiting for him downstairs. But he was determined the next time he took her he wouldn't be like a rutting beast. If only to prove he could wait. If only because it presented a challenge he had to overcome.

Challenges he understood. Challenges he overcame every working day.

It made sense. After rushing their first encounter, and having their second and third cut short, he fully intended to ensure he had all the time in the world the next time. Now all he needed was to find a slot that would accommodate them both.

Maybe after this meeting was done, this interminable meeting where Adrian still seemed hell-bent in holding court...

'Gentlemen,' he interrupted, when there was a break in the traffic and it should have been clear to everyone that this meeting was going nowhere. 'And Miss Turner,' he added, acknowledging Quinn's PA whose ruddy cheeks flared even redder at his unexpected chivalry. 'I think it's time we realized that we've all got too bogged down in the detail. I suggest we take a break and come together again when we're all fresh.'

Weary heads all around the table hesitated before nodding in agreement, and once he was certain he had majority support he followed up with, 'Meanwhile, I invite Stuart Quinn and his wife to dinner tonight. Maybe over a civilized meal and a fine New-Zealand Sauvignon Blanc we can work out where we're both coming from and settle this thing once and for all, before we hand it over to our respective teams to sort out the nuts and bolts?'

Quinn hesitated, his face a scowl before he nodded,

clearly sensing he had Dante on the ropes. 'A good idea,' he huffed. 'Let's say eight o'clock.'

'Good call,' Adrian told him, slapping Dante on the back as they made their way to their waiting car. 'Between the two of us, we'll soon have Quinn begging for mercy.'

Dante stiffened at the unwanted familiarity. 'No,' he said, fixing him with his stare. 'You've got the night off to chase up every possible politician you can get hold of to get to the bottom of that zoning change.'

'But the dinner?'

'I'm taking Mackenzi.'

'But this is our chance to nail him to the wall,' Adrian blustered. 'Two against one. What good will she be?'

'I don't want you there tonight,' Dante told his dumbfounded associate. 'I've told you what I want you to do. Go do it.'

'But—'

'That's all,' he said, dismissing him as he stepped into the waiting car alone. He leaned back into the leather upholstery and stretched his spine. Adrian was becoming more and more of a loose cannon. He was someone Dante had trusted implicitly for years, but maybe too long if his lack of forethought was going to land them in a mess like this. He should never have gone to Ashton House and left Adrian in charge of the Quinn deal at this critical stage. But the thought of owning Ashton House at last was the culmination of a dream so big that he'd wanted to see it first hand, had wanted to visit that place one last time.

Before he wiped it from the face of the earth.

* * *

It was driving her crazy.

Mackenzi paced the living room's long wall of windows, bored to distraction. And getting angrier by the minute. He'd brought her here, insisted she should accompany him, even chased her to her home to ensure she hadn't changed her mind—and all for what? To be left sitting stranded in a hotel suite waiting until *he* had time for her.

Like a good little mistress, she'd browsed the boutiques, the gift store and the jeweller downstairs until she was sick of the sight of one more designer anything, and had taken herself off to wander the windy streets. A sudden rain squall had sent her back to the hotel, and now it was after two in the afternoon, Dante had left before eight and she was going stir crazy. Twenty-four hours since they'd left Adelaide, and still he hadn't made a move on her. Still he kept her waiting.

She threw herself down on the couch, plucking at the tasselled fringe of a cushion before tossing it away dissatisfied, deciding she needed to be up and moving.

So he was busy? Where was the all-conquering, all-powerful invader who'd plundered her when he'd found her asleep in his bed? Where was the ruthless savage who'd threatened to take her roughly yesterday? Had he taken to heart her request not to be taken like an animal? She doubted it. Doubted he even possessed a heart.

No, it was more likely she'd overplayed her hand, protested once too often, and he was over her already. Why else would he have ignored her so completely this morning when he was naked and halfway to being aroused, and she'd lain welcoming in his bed? More likely he'd already decided this was a mistake and he didn't want her, and she wouldn't even get to first base when it came to saving the hotel. He was paying her back, and his PA probably already had her return flight booked.

Damn the man!

Forty minutes later, when she was more strung out than ever, finally there was a sound at the door, the swipe of a card then a click, and he was back. She was ready to be accommodating, ready to forgive, and then he grunted what she guessed was supposed to pass as some kind of greeting when he saw her standing by the window.

It was the final straw. So much for her plans. The caveman was back in his cave, and there was no point trying to reason with a caveman.

She'd given up trying. From now on, just like her, the hotel was on its own.

She headed for the bedroom, tossing off a line she knew he'd hate but, by hell, that he deserved. 'Successful day fending off dinosaurs?'

He growled. He wasn't in the mood for this. He hadn't slept for thirty-something hours, Quinn was playing hardball and smart-mouth Mackenzi wasn't making things any easier. In fact, he was beginning to wonder why he'd brought her along for the ride. As mistresses went, so far she was a major disappointment. He should have taken her in the office when he'd had the chance and tamed her into submission right then and there. Instead he'd given her space.

What the hell had he been thinking? She'd been the one lying in wait in his bed for him, the one who'd responded in flames to his touch, the one who'd agreed to become his mistress. Nobody set conditions on Dante Carrazzo—least of all someone he'd expected to provide nothing more than a few nights' pleasure.

He poured himself a whiskey and threw it back neat, liking the burn, relishing the burst of warmth all the way down. The Quinn deal was in danger of falling apart around his ears—he wasn't used to that—and the only thing that had changed lately was this woman and her constant interruptions into his thoughts. How was he supposed to concentrate on a five-hundred-million dollar deal when his mind was trapped on how he was going to tame a tongue that could slice you apart? There were other things he had planned for that tongue, other things that her current mood told him he wasn't going to be enjoying any time soon.

So much for fantasy.

From the bedroom he heard closet doors banging, the scrape of metal on metal, a thud.

'If it's all the same to you,' he called out, gazing into his glass and already thinking he'd have to make the dinner with Quinn alone, 'I'm not really in the mood for any of your "Neanderthal" rhetoric right now.'

'No?' he heard her say. 'That's too bad. Because I'm not in the mood for social niceties right now.'

'I don't remember ever asking you for social niceties.'

She walked past the open door, a bundle of stuff in her hands. 'Of course. I forgot. You merely expect me to be your mistress.'

He sighed roughly and poured himself another shot. Made it a double. By God, anyone would think they were an old married couple. No wonder he didn't do family.

Dante turned away, staring out the windows, his blood raging, never before having been driven to such insanity by one woman, and more and more forgetting the reasons for choosing this particular woman to accompany him. Where was the woman who'd lain like a temptress in his bed this morning? What had happened to her?

Maybe he should send her home now. After all, he had no intention of changing his mind about the fate of Ashton House, and it wasn't like she was enjoying her part of the bargain.

He angled himself towards the bedroom door. 'You didn't seem to have a problem with agreeing to be my mistress before.'

She flashed past the doorway. 'Well, I've got a problem with it now.' He frowned and took another swig. Two minutes later she passed the doorway again, this time carrying her sponge bag from the bathroom.

What the…? In half a dozen strides he was there, his blood running cold at the sight of her bending over her case on the bed, as she tried to press the mess of belongings in flat enough to close it. 'What are you doing?'

'What's it look like? I'm leaving.'

'Why?'

She zipped up the case, picked up her bag and faced him at the door. The colour was up in her cheeks, her breathing rapid, yet her eyes looked as cold as glacial chips. 'Because this was a mistake. I should never have come. Now, if you'll just let me pass?'

He didn't move, fury turning him rigid. No woman walked away from Dante Carrazzo, not even one he'd already decided to throw out. 'We had a deal. You agreed to this.'

'I didn't agree to sit around all day like some vacuous bimbo, waiting to serve her surly master.'

He leaned in closer to her. 'Plenty of women would enjoy the privilege.'

She stood her ground, only the rise and fall of her chest betraying her quickening breathing. 'I think you're confusing "enjoy" with "endure".'

He growled, his fingers tight around his glass. 'You seemed to enjoy serving me just fine last time.'

She tossed her chin higher, her colour rising. 'I was asleep.'

'Then maybe I should wait until you're asleep,' he suggested. 'You'd be a damned sight less argumentative, for a start.'

'And maybe you should just stop playing this game and get it over with!'

CHAPTER SEVEN

HE'D FLUNG the glass aside and crossed the room in a heartbeat, ignoring the smash of glass as he slammed her against the wall, punching the air from her lungs before she'd even realized what was happening, before she could react. And then his mouth was on her, hot and furious, his hands wild and tearing at her clothes.

Damn it, he'd waited long enough. Put up with *more* than enough. Forget the niceties; blood was pounding in his ears, a tribal beat, a call to action. It was time to show her what she was here for.

Heat met him where he'd been expecting fight. The hungry heat of her mouth, the tangled dance of her tongue, the need radiating out from her like a beacon. He pulled his mouth away long enough to wrench off her top and fill his hands with her breasts, shoving aside her bra in the process. She gasped in his mouth before her teeth found his lip, and he tasted the sharp metallic taste of blood—his blood—while her hands raked through his hair, anchoring him to her.

Her scent was everywhere, her taste filling his senses. He dragged in a breath and drank her in, but it wasn't enough. He dropped his hands to her skirt, sliding down to cup her through the fabric, making her strain against him, and still it was nowhere near close enough.

Need, urgent and unstoppable, filled his very being, powering his actions. Her skirt was no barrier, his hands burrowing beneath, pulling down the scrap of fabric that guarded his ultimate destination, while her hands worked similarly desperately to free him.

He felt himself released, her long fingers greedily circling him, and he gritted his teeth. It was all he could do to hang on. He found her core, slick and sweet and ready, her muscles beckoning, calling to him like a siren's song. And then he lifted her, bracing himself against the wall, curling her legs around him, and gave himself up to his fate.

She gasped as he entered her, her head thrown back, her spine arching as he filled her.

'You like that?' he squeezed out, hanging on himself but watching her, determined to show her denial for what it was.

She uttered something, an indecipherable sound as he eased out of her only to slam into her once again. She shuddered against him, her muscles coming down tight to claim him, to hold him, to keep him.

'Tell me,' he urged. 'Tell me now you don't enjoy this.'

She shook her head, her emerald eyes wild and unseeing. 'No,' she whispered.

He drove into her again and then again. 'Tell me this is something to be endured.' She clung to him, her eyelids fluttering closed. He let his body set the rhythm, taking him closer to the end, closer to where he needed to be.

'Tell me!' he demanded, knowing he wouldn't last much

longer, wanting to punish her for her denials, wanting to exact retribution for making him wait.

Her head lolled back against the wall, damp with perspiration, her breathing coming in gasps as she rode him. 'I can't,' she admitted as her breath hitched on that last word.

He felt the explosion inside her. He felt it tightening all around him, drawing him further inside, until he remembered what it was that had made him want her again and until there was nowhere for him to go. There was nothing that he could do but give into the siren's song and let himself be smashed against the rocks.

It seemed like forever they stayed together like that, pressed hard against the wall, their bodies recovering, no sound but the slowing thump of their heartbeats and the corresponding slowing in their breathing. He lowered her legs and felt her knees buckle as she hit the floor, but he still had her, and a moment later she steadied and he pulled fractionally away—and he saw.

He touched the backs of his fingers to her cheek, blotting the unexpected and baffling moisture. 'You're crying?'

She squeezed her eyes shut, her mouth tightening as she gave a shake of her head.

'Then what's wrong?'

She looked up at him hesitantly, her features tortured, her green eyes wide and glossy like jewels. 'Just…thank you.'

Pride swelled large in his chest. He had her. She was his for as long as he wanted, until he tired of her. And he intended to make the most of it.

It was only when they came apart that he realized. He cursed out loud, slamming his open hand against the wall, cursing himself for the desperation that had seen him forget to use protection. He'd been so blind with rage, goaded by her taunts, and so focused on proving his point that he hadn't been thinking straight.

She jumped, turning her face away, her eyes afraid. 'What is it?'

'I didn't use a condom,' he said, knowing he'd scared her, touching his stinging hand to her cheek. 'Are you protected?'

She nodded dumbly. 'The Pill,' she said, her voice low and half-drowsy in the aftermath of their love-making, her lips swollen and pink and beautiful as she spoke. She frowned a little then, and he couldn't help but smooth her brow with the pad of one finger.

He kissed her because he couldn't resist her lips any more, and smiled at their tender sweetness, thankful that they hadn't both been relying on him for birth control. 'We were both beyond thinking. But, I promise you, that won't happen again.'

He lifted her into his arms and carried her to the large *en suite* bathroom, where he stripped them of the remnants of their clothes and took her into the shower with him. He washed her, exploring with his soaped hands every dip and curve in her flesh. Then he let her soap him down, relishing the fascination in her eyes as she discovered his body, her breasts plump and firm, her nipples tightly beaded, and her eyes rich with the promise of imminent sex.

Then he returned her to their bedroom, depositing her on the wide expanse of their enormous bed, lifting her suitcase to the ground—out of sight, out of mind. This time he made no mistake, retrieving the package from the bedside table.

'Let me,' she asked nervously, and after a momentary

hesitation he allowed her to take the foil package from him and peel it open. He held his breath as she held the tip against his swollen glans and then rolled it down, imprisoning his thrumming length. Then he was sheathed, and it was time to bury himself in yet another warmer embrace.

But first he dipped his head to one dusky nipple and drew it in deep. She arched into his mouth, almost mewing. 'Please,' she begged, parting her legs for him.

He wasn't about to make her wait. He positioned himself above her, taking all the time in the world this time, extracting every last, sweet moment of anticipation from almost joining, until in one fluid stroke he pressed himself home.

And this time it was better, if that were possible, the sheer power of their coupling magnified tenfold. She fitted him so well, her satin skin moving like liquid poetry against him, inciting him to greater heights, greater pleasure. Once again he was reminded of why, after that first night, he'd known he wanted her again. Of why he'd been determined he had to have her.

Because he'd known he had to have her again. He'd known having her with him could work, at least while the fire between them burned bright and strong.

Just like he knew that afterwards, after the fires had burned out and the flames had subsided, things would be different, and he could excise her from his life and go back to complete his plan.

But that would be then. Right now, with her legs curled around him, he wasn't going anywhere.

He reared up, straining, feeling close, needing leverage as her hot mouth left his to trail down his neck. Her lips danced down his neck, doing things with her tongue against his flesh that should be illegal, threatening to bring him undone.

That *did* bring him undone. He exploded into her like a tornado, wild and frenzied and powerful, and she went with him, her own storm merging with his to become one unrelenting maelstrom that sent them both spinning in its wake.

Sweat-slicked and panting, sleep tugging at him, insistent, unrelenting, he moved his mouth up to her neck, tasting soap and salt and one-hundred per cent woman.

'We have a dinner tonight,' he said. 'Wake me at seven.'

Mackenzi showered and unpacked her suitcase quietly, careful not to disturb him until seven o'clock, but in reality relishing the opportunity to watch him sleep. His face was turned away on the pillow, and his arms flung wide, exposing his bare back in all its sculpted perfection.

Would he be cold? She could pull the covers higher, but that might wake him. Besides, then she'd be denied the spectacular view, and right now she couldn't get enough of the sight of him. She tingled anew as she remembered how his skin had felt next to hers, her inner muscles tender and still gently pulsing with the memory of how he'd felt inside her.

It had been better than she remembered. So much better, so much more, the sensations fuelled by hour after hour of anticipation. Hours of frustration.

God, how she'd wanted him! She'd never experienced a hunger like it before, had never forgotten her mind or her purpose with such all-consuming obsession.

She allowed herself a smile as she retrieved her black

beaded dress and slipped it over her head. She didn't feel frustrated any more. On the contrary, she felt alive and replete and sexy as hell, aching in places that wouldn't let her forget what they'd done, and feeling more like a woman than she'd ever felt before.

The weight of the beads pulled the dress into place and she zipped it up, smoothing it over her curves. It seemed a fraction tighter than she remembered, and for a moment she panicked, but then she turned one way and then the other in the full-length mirror and her smile returned— maybe a fraction tighter wasn't such a bad thing.

She twisted her hair up high, softer than she would do it for work, leaving coiling tendrils free to frame her face, before applying make-up. She looked different, she thought as she surveyed the result. Her eyes were lined with kohl, smoky and seductive, and her lips still plumped from their love-making. Even the kink in her nose she hated so much looked less noticeable tonight.

Her smile grew wider. Maybe being a mistress had its good points after all.

And, now that they'd got the sex thing out of the way, she could take a step back and think more rationally about what she was doing here. Dante had seemed to be reasonably happy with her performance, from what she could tell. And if she kept on pleasing him in bed sooner or later she would have the opportunity to talk to him, to make him see the madness in destroying such a beautiful building when it gave pleasure to so many. Maybe she might change his mind after all. She had to face it, she was hardly going to convince him to save Ashton House by a return to acting like she had before.

She was just rezipping her make-up bag when she found them—her strip of birth-control pills—and her fingers fell on them gratefully. She'd told Dante she was on the Pill, so it was just as well that she had remembered. She poured a glass of water and went to pop out the day's pill when she noticed: surely that wasn't the right day...?

She must have missed one. Then came the sickening realization that she'd missed not one but two pills—the first that night in the hotel when she'd stayed over at the hotel unexpectedly, the second when they'd arrived in Auckland so late and she hadn't been thinking straight.

And she'd told him she was protected! She dropped down to the side of the bath. Should she tell him? That would hardly improve her stocks. Or should she wait? There was really no point in worrying him unnecessarily, surely? And something told her it was hardly the thing Dante would take kindly to hearing. Besides, what were the chances? People tried for months to get pregnant, didn't they?

Mackenzi checked her watch. It was time to wake Dante. She stood up, a bit shaky but almost convinced it would be okay, popped two pills and swallowed them down. It would be okay. Life couldn't be that cruel.

She rounded the wide bed and called softly to him. He didn't stir, and she called his name again, louder this time.

His breathing was slow and steady, his eyelids barely flickering as he slept soundly on. He was so beautiful asleep. She sat down on the bed alongside him, leant down with a hand to his strong shoulder, and dipped her face low, drinking in his masculine scent, feeding on it.

Her lips brushed his cheek. 'Dante,' she murmured, and

this time pressed her lips to the corner of his mouth, stroking him, tasting, remembering.

He stirred below her, one arm suddenly snaking around her neck before she could pull away, his mouth now moving under hers in a sensual play of flesh against flesh, the sensations pulling at her like a drug, demanding more. Then, with one powerful toss of his body, he rolled her until she was under him and it was his turn to take advantage of her mouth, heady and intoxicating and deep.

How long the kiss lasted, she had no idea. She'd lost all concept of time, abandoned all notion of preserving her make-up. All she knew was that when finally he pulled away she was breathless and dizzy and more turned on than any woman had a right to be, especially a woman who had climaxed twice already today.

His face hovered above her own, his eyes heavy with desire. 'Now *that's* what I call a wake-up call. You look…good enough to eat.' Then he frowned, his brow puckering. 'How long have we got?'

Excitement skittered up her spine anew, obliterating any concerns about missed pills and chances. 'Long enough.'

He smiled, and his mouth headed back for a repeat performance. 'That's the right answer,' he said before destroying her make-up some more.

'Stuart Quinn is owner and CEO of Quinn Boatbuilding Enterprises here in Auckland,' Dante explained during their limo ride to the restaurant. They were running almost to time for their eight o'clock dinner appointment, which was a minor miracle given the amount of repair work she'd had to do when Dante had finally released her.

'Quinn,' he continued, 'owns a rare two-hundred metre strip of prime harbour-front property in an area ripe for re-development. His business is floundering, in serious need of updating. He lacks the cash to retool, can't get finance, but is pulling out all stops to circumvent a sale to me—even to the point of getting his cronies to stand in the way of zoning changes that would see my development-proposal accepted.'

'Why can't he get a loan? The land alone must be worth a fortune.'

'He's borrowed heavily against it already to support his son's ailing business, a gamble that failed. The bank won't extend any more credit.'

She frowned. 'How do you know that?'

'Simple. I own a controlling interest in his bank.'

'So what—you pulled the rug out from under his feet?'

'The bank needs to make a profit for its shareholders, of which I am one. Bad risks need not apply.'

'Oh, for heaven's sake, couldn't you at least have given him a fighting chance?'

'Look, I didn't get where I am by waiting for people to hand me something on a plate. It doesn't work that way. I believe that if you want something in this world, you have to go after it. And if you blow your chances you don't deserve it. It's winner takes all.'

Mackenzi settled back into the upholstery, starkly reminded of how utterly ruthless Dante Carrazzo could be. She felt uncomfortable with the fact she'd even needed the reminder, when just a short time ago she'd been totally fixated on how good he made her feel, how good he felt inside her, and was already anticipating their next en-counter, his ruthlessness the furthest thing from her mind.

But the wild and passionate lover had another passionate side—a side that saw him determined to win in business at all costs—and it would be at her own peril to forget it. 'So you ensure Quinn is without financing, and he ensures you don't get zoning approval. Sounds like you both deserve each other.'

Alongside her Dante made a sound like a growl. 'All that concerns you is that tonight he's bringing his wife, Christine. Just be charming and keep Christine amused, and I get the chance to work on the old man.'

'Turn the screws, you mean.'

'I prefer to think of it as persuading him to see reason.'

'I bet you do. So will Adrian be there?'

He looked around. 'Why do you ask?'

It was her turn to look away. She gazed out of her window, feigning an interest in the view and the lights playing on the dark waters of the harbour as they neared their destination. 'I thought with him being your second in charge and all…'

'No,' he told her. 'Adrian won't be there.'

She breathed a sigh of relief. There was something about the man that rubbed her up the wrong way, and he'd made no secret of the fact he thought even less of her. Not having him around would be one less source of tension tonight. The car came to a halt outside the plush harbourside restaurant, sails and skilful lighting transforming the courtyard entry into a look reminiscent of a yacht in full sail.

Stuart and Christine Quinn were already seated at the bar, waiting for them. Stuart was a sprightly senior with snowy-white hair and crinkled skin, but with eyes still rapier sharp. Christine was all elegance in a powder-blue suit encrusted with seed pearls, smile lines the only visible signs of aging in her pleasant face. Mackenzi warmed to her immediately.

'What an unusual name for a woman,' Christine said honestly after the introductions were made. 'I don't think I've ever heard of that one before.'

'It's an old family name,' Mackenzi told her. 'Usually the province of first-born boys.'

'And your parents decided to break with tradition?'

'Sort of. They struggled to have a child at all. I was an IVF baby, and my parents decided that they may never get another chance, and so went with tradition even though their first born was a girl. They dropped the "e" off the end and gave me Rose as a second name, just so I had something feminine to go with it.'

'Mackenzi Rose,' Christine said, nodding as if testing the names on her tongue. 'Well, I like it. Individual and feminine. I think it suits you too.'

A few minutes more small-talk later, they were ushered to their table, looking out through a wall of glass over the moonlit harbour, the lights of houses across the water twinkling in the distance.

'So tell me, just what are we doing here tonight, Dante?' Stuart Quinn asked after they'd ordered, his voice gruff and gravelly. 'I thought it was pretty clear at today's meeting that negotiations are at stalemate.'

Beside her Mackenzi sensed Dante tense, caught his tight no-nonsense smile. 'I always believe there's a solution to everything. I'm sure we can get around this stalemate if we just come at it from a different angle.'

'But I don't want to sell to you, not if you're going to

pull down the boatyard and replace it with row upon row of those apartment buildings of yours. If you thought that showing up here with a beautiful woman on your arm was going to suddenly make me change my mind about that, then you must think I've gone soft in the head. That boatyard has been there for almost seventy-five years. Generations of employees have worked there. It deserves more than to be wiped off the face of the earth.'

Dante's lips thinned until Mackenzi was sure there wasn't a drop of blood left in them. 'So why don't you just take the money I'm offering and relocate?'

'Why should I, when I have the perfect location on the harbour right now?'

Dante flicked his napkin down on the table. 'Why should this dinner be anything to do with the deal?'

'Isn't it?' Quinn turned to Mackenzi, obviously aware there was no such thing as a free meal. 'So tell me, young lady, what's your role in all this tonight? Are you going to try to butter me up and convince me that I should be doing business with Dante Carrazzo at all costs?'

There was a startled, 'Stuart!' from Christine at the same time as laser-sharp eyes latched onto her own.

'On the contrary,' Mackenzi said without a glimmer of remorse, 'from my experience dealing with Dante, personally I think you're wise to hang out for a better deal. Even if that means dealing with someone else.'

She felt the heat of Dante's eyes turn on her, not failing to notice the simmering warning contained therein.

'Do you, indeed?' Stuart said. 'And what kind of deal do you think I should be holding out for?'

She looked at the faces around the table nervously.

'Forgive me, this probably sounds crazy, but from the little information I have heard I'm wondering if there isn't something in the proposed redevelopment for both of you.'

Quinn's hand flew through the air. 'I'm not interested in apartment blocks. And the zoning changes won't allow for a residential component that high. As far as I'm concerned, Carrazzo here can't do anything with the land zoned the way it is, not with his current plans.'

'Then maybe he should change them. Why not share the redevelopment? From the sounds of it, there's more than enough land, surely, for a new state-of-the-art boatyard together with an apartment complex. Maybe even a marina between them, to tie the whole development together. Why not go into it as partners, rather than adversaries? That way nobody loses and you can both benefit. Surely there would be synergistic benefits? And Dante would have more chance of winning the goodwill of the regulatory bodies.'

'Mackenzi,' Dante interrupted, 'that's enough.' He turned to Quinn. 'Like Mackenzi said, she knows nothing of the detail about the project.'

Quinn ignored him, and continued to regard her speculatively, his fingers steepled in front of him. 'You're certainly not what I was expecting, young lady. For what it's worth, your idea could certainly be one way around the mixed-zoning issue. The trouble is, Carrazzo and I are both what you might call lone wolves when it comes to business. Even if the figures stacked up, I don't know that a collaboration could work. What do you think, Carrazzo?'

She turned to the man at her side. His jaw was working grimly, his eyes like stone, and Mackenzi knew she'd way overstepped the role he'd assigned her for the evening. 'I think,' he said at last, 'that perhaps we should forget about the deal for a while and enjoy our meal.'

'What the hell was that all about?'

Dinner had concluded, a pleasant enough evening if one could ignore the simmering wariness that had marked the two battling sides. It was a pity it had been impossible to ignore it. Dante had been silent during the journey back to the hotel, striding through the lobby like a lion unleashed while she'd battled to keep up in his wake. Now he stood there, a glass of malt whiskey in one hand, leaning on the credenza with the other.

'What was what about?'

'That suggestion for collaboration—where did that come from?'

She shrugged, dropping her beaded bag onto the coffee table, and stretched her neck this way and that, trying to ease some of the tension that had gathered there in the last few hours. 'I don't know. It just seemed the logical thing to do. Quinn needs funds to upgrade an iconic boat–building business that's missing out on contracts because it can't retool, given you've put a stop on finance—and meanwhile you merely want to turn the land into some kind of waterfront-apartment desert. Why not build some-thing bigger than just another set of apartment buildings, something that builds on and also preserves a business that's been part of the harbour-front for the better part of a century?'

'I'm not in the business of boat building.'

'Tell me something I don't know. You're so obviously not in the business of building anything!'

'That's garbage. I've built an entire fortune. From nothing!'

'To what end? So you can pull down and destroy every iconic property you can lay your hands on? How many hotels have you already destroyed?'

'I built on those sites—'

'What—more of your characterless concrete apartment-blocks? That wasn't building. That was merely sticking band-aids over the scars you'd left behind. And now you've got both Ashton House and Quinn Boatbuilding lined up in your sights.'

'Ashton House has got nothing to do with Quinn Boatbuilding!'

'Hasn't it? You seem so determined to destroy everything you touch—'

'Did you hear me? I said *nothing*!'

She blinked, wondering at the raw emotion she saw behind his eyes, the depths of emotion that lay behind that statement, wondering what it meant for her quest. 'Which means what, exactly? How are they different, then?'

He turned away. 'Believe it. They are.'

She took a reluctant step closer, wanting to know. Needing to know. 'I don't understand.'

'And I don't understand why you made that suggestion to Quinn in the first place. I expect more from someone who's supposed to be on my team.'

'I was on *your* team until you made me redundant, remember? Now I'm working on *my* team, to get what *I* want.'

'And what is it you want—to undermine my negotiations when they're already at a critical stage?'

'You know damn well what I want. To stop you destroying Ashton House. To make you see the madness of doing so.'

He shook his head slowly from side to side as he came closer, the look on his face coldly triumphant. 'No, it's not. You like to think you're here for some noble reason, but I know what you really want. You've made that patently clear over the last twenty-four hours, with your taunts and your goading and your all-too-innocent attempts at seduction. That's what you were trying to do this morning when you let the covers slip so innocently to show off your cleavage. A pity you were wearing your neck-to-knees pyjamas when it was clear you were trying to lure me into your bed!'

She was shaking her head at everything he said, shocked at the veracity contained in his statements, shocked that he had read her so well, not wanting to believe her need had been so transparent.

'And when it didn't work,' he continued, 'you got desperate and figured that, if you made out you were leaving, I'd get angry enough to want to stop you. As I did, to our mutual benefit.'

'No,' she said, truthfully this time. 'I *was* leaving. I'd had enough.'

'But you hadn't had *any*! That's what was really bugging you, wasn't it? Admit it, Mackenzi, you're not here to save anything—not Ashton House, not the world. You're here because you want me in your bed. Against the wall. Any way you can damn well get it!'

CHAPTER EIGHT

HIS COARSE WORDS slashed her like a knife, because he was so wrong. She wanted to save Ashton House—it was the reason she was here, the reason she'd agreed to this crazy deal in the first place.

Yet at the same time he was so right. Because she had been prepared to walk away—to flee—and to leave Ashton House to its fate when she hadn't been able to take the pressure-cooker tension of waiting for him to make her his mistress any more. To make her feel as good again as he had that first night together.

'You can believe whatever you like,' she whispered. 'But I tell you one thing—whatever I'm here for, it's not to save your damned deal. If you're so dead set on destroying any business that stands in your way, that you can't see the potential good in collaborating with Quinn rather than wiping his business of the face of the earth, you don't deserve to be in business.'

'You don't know the first thing about it.'

'I know that someone should at least have costed the proposal. My gut feeling is that if you can come up with a waterfront proposal that features a new and improved

Quinn Boatbuilding organisation as an integral part of the harbour-front design and attach it to a marina, you're going to have interest from every boatie in town—plus the endorsement of every regulatory body going, because you've taken care of one of their own.'

'You're guessing.'

'Of course I'm guessing. I don't have the numbers. But I suspect that if you play your cards right you'll probably be able to ask double for your precious apartments, even if you do end up with planning permission for only half as many. Financially it may be a different kind of deal from what you originally envisaged, but there's a chance with any future profits from Quinn Boatbuilding that you'll come out way ahead. And, let's face it, how else are you going to get around the zoning regulations? Quinn certainly seemed to think it might work.'

'He was humouring you.'

'Is that so? Well, at least he damned well listened and didn't put me down in the process. But you're probably right, and, let's face it, Quinn's probably much better off having nothing to do with you. And now, if you excuse me, it's been a very long night. I'm going to bed.'

Dante made a move towards her, unbuttoning his collar and pulling his tie askew in the process. 'That's the first sensible thing you've said all night.'

Heat scorched her cheeks as he came closer. She reeled back, her senses on red alert. He had to be kidding! Despite the veracity in the accusations he'd earlier charged her with—the frustration she'd felt waiting for him to make a move, the utter desperation when he hadn't—there was no way in the world he was coming anywhere near her tonight.

And it wasn't just his total disregard for her ideas, it was the impression he gave her that she had no right to have any ideas, that her role began and ended in his bed. She jagged up her chin with a note of defiance. 'I meant *alone*.'

'So did I.' He tossed back the rest of his whiskey and turned away, heading for the office. 'Go put your flannelette defences up. And don't wait up.'

She didn't wait up. Not intentionally. She wasn't waiting for anyone, she told herself as she tossed and turned in the wide, lonely bed. *Especially not him.*

Yet sleep still eluded her, her body too hot under too much cover, her mind in turmoil over a man who was such a contradiction. A man who went from ruthless tycoon to passionate lover and back again without giving her time to either catch her breath or guard her emotions. A man she didn't want.

So why did it sting so much that he hadn't wanted her?

Dante opened his laptop and dug out the files he had on the deal and the financials he had on Quinn's operation. Mackenzi had no idea what she was talking about, and he'd damn well prove it to her. He had to, in case Quinn got it into his head that she'd been on to something and made it even harder for them to close the deal.

It was hard enough already, given Adrian's disaster with the zoning regulations; he didn't need any more complications. He spread the development plans out on the desk alongside him, weighting down the corners with paperweights as the files loaded—page upon page filled with numbers, calculations, projected costs and revenue streams—and got to work.

It was almost dawn by the time he pushed back his chair from the desk, his work done as the first hint of light formed a grey smudge around the blinds.

He sipped at the strong coffee room service had just delivered and pulled the curtain sash, revealing a city shrugging off the night. It had rained some time during the night, the clouds hanging low over the city. Street cleaners patrolled the gutters many floors below, their yellow lights flashing. Beyond them he could see the motorways, now flowing freely, soon to become choked and snarled, and beyond them the harbour, the heart and soul of Auckland, a piece of Auckland he wanted a share in.

And today, come hell or high water, he'd make it happen.

He snapped open his mobile phone and hit an oft-used code. It answered on the third ring.

'Adrian, have you got what I wanted?'

'I'm working on it,' his second-in-charge said, with just a hint of tiredness in his voice. 'There's a politician I'm meeting with later today, to see if he'll pull some strings on the re-zoning.'

'So you've got nothing.'

There was a pause at the end of the line. 'Like I said, I'm working on it. These things take time.'

'We don't have time. Cancel it.'

'What did you say?'

'Cancel the meeting,' Dante told him. 'I need you to do something else…'

She hadn't slept well, he could tell from the way she'd launched the pillows all over the bed and tangled herself in both the sheets. And her hair—it half-covered her face now, coiling around her neck, its curled ends spiralling lower.

Tantalisingly lower.

He dragged in a lungful of air, clearing a head still too full of discounted cash-flows and projected rates of return, only to find her perfume curl inside him, warm and welcoming, beckoning him, and turning the figures into a blur. He looked down at her sleeping form as he unbuttoned his shirt, feeling himself stir, already anticipating that first unbeatable contact of skin against skin, a prelude to the delicious slide of flesh against flesh.

Or, he grimaced, flesh against flannelette. Wherever she'd found those crazy pyjamas they were little defence against him.

Would she still be angry with him when she woke up? Damn him to hell, but half of him hoped she was. There was something to be said for anger, especially when it turned a mere mistress into a tigress. And, whatever he'd been expecting from taking Mackenzi as his mistress, he hadn't been expecting the tigress she'd proved herself to be.

He purred softly as he shucked off the rest of his clothes. She was beautiful, awake or asleep, from her slightly crooked nose to her painted toenails. Angry or not, she was still his mistress, and he intended to make the most of her.

He slid into the bed alongside her, propped up on one elbow, drinking in her sleeping body-heat and nestling close. He put a hand to her hip, unable to resist tracing the sensual curve to the sweet dip at her waist and back again. She stirred, untangling herself from her hair, her vivid green eyes blinking open, first slowly as sleep slid away and then widely with surprise.

She reared away from him, her eyes now flashing and wary, circled by shadows that confirmed her lack of sleep. But he held her in place, his hand anchoring her where she lay. And then he leaned over and lightly kissed her startled mouth.

She surveyed him suspiciously, her hands already working the bedclothes higher in defence. 'What was that for?'

'That's to say thank you.'

Her eyes narrowed. 'Why?'

'Because I think you might just have saved this deal.'

It was her turn to prop herself up on her elbows, but her expression was guarded, her eyes still harbouring the remnants of last night's hostility. She shook her head, brushing hair back from her face with one hand. 'You're kidding.'

He shook his head. 'No. It could be tight, but it's definitely workable. Adrian's scheduling a meeting with Quinn later today.'

She said nothing for a while, just stared at him. Then, 'That's nice. I'm happy for Stuart Quinn and the people who work for him. I think.'

He hauled in a breath and forced it out again, his teeth gritted, but knowing he could expect little more after the browbeating he'd given her. 'I should have listened to you,' he admitted, letting his hand move rhythmically under her pyjamas and over that curve from her hip to her waist and back again. 'I should at least have given you a fair hearing.'

'Yes.'

His hand swept up her side, his fingers brushing the underside of her breast, another seductive curve. Air hissed through her teeth but she didn't pull away, so he ventured back, letting his fingertips trace the swell of her breast. Her breathing was quickening now, her green eyes showing the merest hint of desire.

'And, I know you don't have to make this easy for me, but what I'm trying to say is I'm sorry. I was wrong.'

'You're apologizing? To me?'

He smiled. 'Don't spread it around.' He cupped her breast in his hand, felt the tight nub of nipple pressing into his palm and wanted more. He shrugged down the covers, pushed up her top and dipped his mouth to one dusky nipple. 'I wasn't sure Mackenzi suited you,' he said. 'But Rose does. It suits these…' And he turned his attentions to the other.

She gasped. 'What time is it?'

'Getting on for six,' he whispered, his lips dancing over the tip while his hand toyed lazily with its neighbour, rolling it gently between finger and thumb.

He caught her fractured breath, the involuntary arch of her back that accompanied it as his tongue circled its prey.

'And you're just coming to bed?'

'Yes.'

'You worked through the night again?'

He filled his mouth with her, drawing her in, releasing her ever so slowly from the heated embrace of his mouth, his hand now venturing southwards towards another even greater goal. 'Guilty.'

'And you're quite sure you're not a bat?'

He laughed, a low and deep rumble against her breast, suckling at her flesh as her body moved seductively under his, then grazing her satiny skin with his teeth.

'Quite sure,' he assured her as his fingers worked at

edging her pyjamas lower, insinuating themselves between her thighs. 'So, do you accept my apology?'

There was the slightest hint of resistance. 'I don't know.'

His mouth travelled a line from her breasts to her throat, finding a pulse point, feeling the frantic drumbeat of her heart under his mouth, and his tongue lapped it up. 'Can I help make up your mind?'

She pushed her head back into the pillows as she parted her legs for him. 'You can try…'

The phone woke her, Dante answering with a terse, 'Yes?' as he threw his legs over the side of the bed and sat up.

Bleary eyed, she glanced at the clock, finding it already after ten. She collapsed back into the pillows, tiredness from a restless night followed by a passionate awakening still dragging at her. But the memories of that awakening brought a satisfied smile to her face. How could it be possible that the sex could keep getting better when it had been so good to start with? But it *was* better, and he'd been so tender and sweet and genuinely remorseful, a different Dante Carrazzo from the one she thought she knew.

She escaped to the bathroom while he was busy, aghast at how wanton she looked, her hair wild and untamed, her lips rosy and plump, and her breasts still bearing the brand of his whiskered chin. She looked a thorough mess. She looked utterly seduced.

As she had been, she knew, turning on the shower. She'd been seduced by a master of seduction, a man who had seduced an acceptance of his apology out of her. And she'd told herself just last night she didn't want him! Who was she trying to kid? She needed him for the power of life or death he held over Ashton House, but she wanted him for herself.

Mackenzi let the massaging thrum-beat of water cascade over her. Was that so wrong? Why couldn't they both enjoy each other for as long as this arrangement lasted? All she had to do was keep her wits about her. And she was sensible. She always had been, and she certainly wasn't about to fall in love with another totally wrong man. She'd made that mistake once already. At least this one wasn't going to get away with telling her she was frigid.

The shower's massage-setting wove its magic on her scalp and skin, and she emerged in a fluffy white robe ten minutes later feeling refreshed, her skin tingling. He was still on the phone; she could tell that this time he was talking to Quinn, and he looked up at her and smiled, holding up crossed fingers.

Her heart gave a funny little lurch that stopped her in her tracks and she turned, uncertain, fleeing straight back into the bathroom.

He found her there a few minutes later. 'Are you all right? You looked like you'd seen a ghost.'

She offered him a quick smile and made a play of towel-drying her hair. 'Perfectly,' she lied, though at least her heart-rate was something approximate to normal again. Which in this man's proximity meant erratic at best. Especially when, like now, he was naked. How was a girl supposed to think when faced by that unashamed display of potent masculinity?

'Good,' he said, oblivious to her reaction, turning on the shower behind her. 'Because Quinn wants to take us all out in his boat today. He's excited about the new deal, but he's insisting you're there.'

She nodded, wondering both at his choice of words and at the words he hadn't chosen, and wishing she wasn't—because that would mean she cared, and she didn't. She'd convinced herself of that while she'd deep-breathed her heartrate back to some kind of normality. Whatever she'd felt, whatever had struck her when Dante had smiled at her, had been an aberration. A mistake. 'I like Stuart Quinn,' she said on her way out of the bathroom. 'I'd love to go.'

'Oh,' he called as she pulled the door closed behind her. 'And I've ordered something for you from room service. It should be here soon.'

Just as well, she thought as she rifled through her thin wardrobe, because thanks to that morning's activities she was starving. Meanwhile she settled on trousers again and another knit top. There was nothing else, and she wasn't sure what one wore boating anyway. Before she'd finished dressing, their room service arrived, a trolley full of domed dishes, myriad bewitching scents wafting invitingly. Mackenzi's stomach growled.

The waiter set the still-covered platters on the dining table, poured them both coffee and left them to it as Dante joined her, wrapped up in a matching white robe fresh from his shower, his dark hair tousled and still beaded with water at the ends. My God, she thought, once again feeling the effects of a rush of adrenaline to her heart as he came closer. The white of his robe was a stark contrast to his dark features and olive skin. He could have been the model in any number of advertisements, from shavers to toothpaste to aftershave, and he'd have had women lining up to buy the product. He looked so good, so real, one-hundred per cent pure, unadulterated male.

'Hungry?' he asked as he pulled up a chair.

'Starving.'

'Then perhaps,' he said, gesturing towards the half-dozen domed lids, 'you might like to do the honours?'

Clearly she was supposed to be impressed by the feast he'd ordered, but she really didn't give a toss, given how hungry she was. Still, she'd play the game, if only it meant she could eat. She removed the first lid and found a plate of scrambled eggs with salmon, and under the second a heaped high stack of crispy bacon and mushrooms. There were pancakes under the third, with a bowl of rich red strawberries and a jar of syrup, and it was all so special she was practically drooling by the time she lifted the fourth. But this time it was nothing she'd ever seen on a room-service tray.

'What's this?' she asked tightly as she put the lid aside, her concentration focused on the flat box sitting on the silver tray, a new fear unfurling in her gut. 'Dante?'

'A surprise,' he said. 'Open it.'

She shook her head. 'I don't understand.'

'Just open it.'

With shaky fingers she picked it up, her mouth dry, her hunger pangs forgotten as she eased the hinged top up. Only to meet the most perfect emerald pendant she had ever seen, large and emerald-cut, surrounded by what looked like diamonds and suspended from a thin golden band. Matching earrings nestled either side.

She shook her head, frowning. 'I don't understand. Where did it come from?'

'A simple matter to have it delivered from the jewellery store downstairs. Take it,' he urged. 'It's nothing.'

'It's hardly nothing! It's magnificent. Tell me they're not real?'

He was at her side, taking the necklace from the box and leaning down to fix it at her throat. She tingled all over as his warm fingers brushed against her hair and throat, while the gem fell, heavy and cool, against her skin. She traced the stone's generous outline with her fingertips as he gently slid each earring home, transforming her earlobes into erogenous zones. Then he took her hand, pulling her from her chair and across the room to the large gilt-framed mirror on the wall, where he stood with his hands on his hips just behind her, looking over her shoulder at her reflection. 'I wanted something that matches your eyes,' he said, pulling her hair out of the way. 'Do you like them?'

The jewels winked and glittered back at her, any movement reflecting yet another dazzling facet of the stones, their colour indeed complementing the colour of her eyes, heightening it. How much would such a collection be worth? Too much, she knew. And accepting it would cost her even more.

'They're lovely,' she admitted. 'But it's hardly the point.'

'That's entirely the point,' he said, running his hands up her arms to her shoulders, and dipping his head down to kiss her throat. 'You're my mistress. Why shouldn't I spoil you? Especially when you've just resuscitated a deal in imminent danger of collapse.'

His hands felt warm on her shoulders, her skin still tingled from the caress of his lips, and yet his words washed through her like iced water. So the jewels were her fee for services rendered?

It was so wrong. A gift this precious deserved to be given in love. Otherwise it was hollow, its worth devalued.

Her worth devalued.

She might have agreed to be his mistress, but she didn't want or need the trimmings. It wasn't the payback she was looking for.

'Dante, they're beautiful,' she admitted, and for a moment she saw victory reflected on his features. 'But I really can't take it. I didn't agree to this deal so you could shower me with gifts, and if you're suddenly feeling generous there's something I'd much rather have.' She moved away from him, unhooking the necklace and replacing it back in the box along with the earrings.

He watched her in the mirror, his eyes growing colder, his jaw setting firmer. 'And that is?'

She looked at him standing there, his back still to her, his stance tense and unmoving, the calm before the storm. 'You know why I'm here. You promised me you'd rethink your decision about Ashton House's future.'

He swung around, gesturing towards the box she still held in her hands. 'And that precludes me from giving you anything else?'

'It means I won't be bought off with any consolation prizes.'

'You think I'm buying you off?'

'Aren't you? Look, Dante, it's saving Ashton House that's important to me, not some meaningless trinket I get for sleeping with you.'

'Meaningless trinket.' His voice was flatter than the box he removed from her hands, ditching it back onto its platter with a total disregard for its worth that had her shuddering.

'So maybe you could let me know if you're any closer to making a decision,' she ventured cautiously.

He slammed himself back in his chair. 'No.'

'You won't tell me, or you're no closer?'

'I'll let you know when I've made my decision. Now, eat your breakfast. It's getting cold.'

Nowhere near as cold as Dante, that was a fact. She nibbled around the edges of food that tasted of nothing, her appetite banished, while he sat there looking for all the world as if he'd been chiselled from a rock. It had been his deal, yet he was acting like she had a nerve to remind him of it.

Too bad. She wasn't likely to stop reminding him of it, now or any time soon.

CHAPTER NINE

THE MORNING'S dark clouds had rolled away and for now the water of Auckland's Waitemata Harbour sparkled and danced under the afternoon sun. The powerful launch skipped along at a fast pace, and Mackenzi relished being outside with the feel of fresh air whipping around her face, the salt spray turning to jewels in the sunlight. No wonder they called it 'the city of sails', she thought as she looked around, the spectacular harbour dotted with all kinds of sailing craft.

When the air turned cooler Christine and Mackenzi took refuge in the saloon area, enjoying the rich, wooden tones of the teak flooring and the sumptuous upholstery. If this was boating, Mackenzi was hooked.

Dante stood alongside Quinn at the helm, listening intently to him over the thrum of the engines, and every now and then Mackenzi caught the odd word—horsepower, diesel and hydraulics—that told her they were talking about boats and boating design. Dante certainly wasn't wasting any time catching up on his latest investment interest. Just to one side of them, looking like he longed to be part of the *tête-à-tête* but the body language showing he in no way fit in, stood Adrian, scowling with every word.

They slowed when they came to a sandy shore on Motuihe Island, one of the numerous small islands dotting the harbour, the boat now bobbing gently as staff went ahead to offload a picnic lunch on the grassy slopes beyond the beach. It was sheltered here from the wind, making the perfect sun-trap, the perfect picnic-spot.

'It's an impressive launch,' Dante said as they prepared to disembark along the short jetty.

'That's why I wanted you to see it. This prototype is just an indication of what we can do, once the retooling goes ahead. Until that happens, we don't have the means to manufacture enough to achieve the necessary economies of scale.'

'And the amount needed for a complete retooling?'

Quinn rattled off a figure that made Mackenzi's head spin and Adrian's brow furrow, but she noticed Dante barely blinked. Clearly he'd had that figure or close to it in mind when he'd pored over the numbers last night.

'I must say,' Quinn added as they settled around the picnic table, 'I wasn't overly surprised to get your call this morning. I knew you weren't the sort that gave up easily, but I certainly didn't expect you to come out advocating the proposal you did. I thought you'd closed your mind last night to anything to do with incorporating the boat-building business into the redevelopment.'

Dante leaned back, one leg tucked nonchalantly under his chair, the other stretched out in front of him, and threw Mackenzi a look. Even though his eyes were obscured by sunglasses, and despite the tension that had descended on them since that earlier brunch, still her insides did that strange rollover she'd encountered coming out of the bathroom that morning. 'I thought I wasn't keen either, but something kept nagging at me.'

Adrian's scowl grew deeper while Quinn laughed out loud, following Dante's gaze, and giving a crusty wink. 'Tell me, Mackenzi,' he said. 'What's your background? Given your interest in the subject, I'm guessing it's got something to do with the property industry?'

'Mackenzi managed a hotel in Adelaide,' Dante interceded.

She smiled, wondering why becoming Dante's mistress automatically made him her spokesman. 'That's right.' She smiled innocently at him. 'Though right now I'm between jobs, isn't that right, Dante?' She turned to Christine before he had a chance to answer. 'And it was actually a wonderful hotel in the Adelaide Hills called Ashton House. Maybe you might have heard of it?'

'Oh, I know the one,' said Christine. 'You remember, Stuart? We went to the Lennon-Groves' wedding in the gardens there. Some years back. A beautiful wedding. Such a stunning location.'

Quinn's brow creased before he nodded, his face relaxing into a wide smile. 'Of course, pretty spot. Those views were something else.'

Mackenzi allowed herself a 'take that' smile, noticing Dante's expression tighten measurably behind his sunglasses. 'It is a very special place,' she agreed, hoping Dante would eventually get the message. *Far too special to suffer the fate Dante had planned.* 'I was there for three wonderful years. Though, before I did my hospitality-industry training, I worked for a couple of years with a small property business that redeveloped all kinds of dead-end properties into niche sites. I guess it sparked my interest in the industry.'

'Aha,' pronounced Quinn. 'That explains it. Well, given you're between jobs as you say, let me know if you're looking for work in the industry, because I'm sure that I've got some contacts who could use your talents here in Auckland.'

'Thank you, I appreciate it.'

'I don't think she'll have the time,' Dante broke in, snapping his gaze away to focus on Stuart. 'Mackenzi's going to be busy helping me out on a few projects for the foreseeable future.'

She was? She blinked up at him, grateful that her own dark glasses hid her surprise, while Adrian made a sound like a snort and turned away, looking out to sea.

Quinn laughed. 'I should have assumed you'd get in first. Now, how about we enjoy this lunch?'

The Quinns proved entertaining hosts, the atmosphere a world away from their tense dinner together the previous evening. With the combination of good food, sea and sun it proved to be a relaxing couple of hours, sitting out near the water. Mackenzi took in the ever-changing view, choosing to wander along the narrow sandy beach while the others enjoyed coffee and talked about boats. The tiny hairs on her arms told her the instant she had company, standing to attention like soldiers standing guard. She didn't look at him, preferring the view over the water to the sandy beach and bushy shoreline opposite. It was safer that way.

'You're going to have to try harder than that if you want to save your precious Ashton House.'

She took a deep breath and tasted salt and sea, and a man

called Dante, could smell the rich, dark coffee he held in his hands. She'd been expecting some kind of reaction over her mention of Ashton House, and his voice sounded low and threatening enough—but where was the venom she'd been expecting? Was he mellowing? She doubted it. His restraint had more to do with business and a deal he didn't want to risk losing again. He could hardly make a scene with Quinn hovering.

'I didn't realize I was trying anything,' she said ingenuously. 'You were the one who brought up the topic of me managing the hotel. I was merely expanding on it.'

He didn't respond, and she could have lost herself again in the gentle slap of water along the shore, the cry of a wheeling gull and the occasional burst of laughter from the lunch party. *Could* have lost herself, if not for the man standing so close beside her.

'Are you sure you wouldn't like a coffee?'

'I don't think I could fit another thing in,' she said without looking around. It was the truth. Whether it was the sea air or the more relaxed atmosphere after their strained brunch, she'd more than made up for her earlier lack of appetite.

'You never told me you'd worked in the property development industry.'

'I don't recall you ever asking.' Only then did she turn from the view and look at him, having to raise her chin because of his height and because he was standing so close. 'And what's this about me helping you out on a few projects?'

Dante gave a careless shrug of his shoulders, the open neck of his white shirt rippling with the motion and drawing her attention to that eye-level triangle of olive skin and its dusting of dark, coiling hair. 'It wouldn't be too much trouble to give me your opinion when I ask for it, would it?'

She smiled and allowed her eyes to wander slowly back up. 'My, my. Now you're asking my opinion. I have come up in the world.'

'I wouldn't think too much about it,' he countered, picking up a stray tendril of her hair and winding it around his finger until she was drawn to him like a fish on a reel. A fish that had too easily given up the will to fight; it occurred to her too late. 'It's simply a matter of making the most of our arrangement.'

He frowned slightly and touched a fingertip to her nose, running over the slight sideways bump. She tried to pull away but her hair around his finger kept her right there, tingling under his touch. 'What happened here?'

'I broke it playing hockey,' she said, embarrassed and putting a hand up self-consciously. 'It never set quite straight.'

'I like it,' he said, surprising her. 'It's got character. A bit like you.'

They stood that way together on the beach, not touching but for the finger still coiled tight in her hair and keeping her head angled up towards him. His lips slightly turned up at the corners, his eyes smoky with desire. Mackenzi felt the answering effects deep inside her, where heat pooled low between her thighs in time with the gentle ebb and flow of the water along the beach and the thumping drumbeat of her heart.

He was flirting with her, she realized, seducing her with barely a touch right here on the shore in full view of anyone and everyone. Despite everything she knew about him, despite every reason she knew she shouldn't play his game, she wasn't about to stop him. Not when it made her feel like this.

It was just a game, she reminded herself, just a game. It was about strategy and tactics and keeping your head. All she had to do was keep her head.

Then he looked down at her lips and she lost it. He was going to kiss her. Her lips parted in answer, a silent consent, and on her next breath she could taste the very essence of him, feeling it coil all the way down.

'Excuse me, Dante.'

Dante didn't move a muscle, his eyes remaining locked on her mouth. 'What is it, Adrian?' His words came short and sharp.

'Quinn's suggesting that we get our teams together tonight over a working dinner to brief them on the new arrangements.'

'Good idea,' Dante agreed, still without turning his head.

'I'll let him know.' Adrian turned to go.

This time Dante moved, releasing the tension in her hair and her body like a switch, letting the coils of her hair slide away just as the coils inside her diminished. 'And, Adrian?'

His second-in-charge stopped like an eager puppy who'd been denied attention for too long. 'Yes?'

'Book yourself a seat on the first flight back to Melbourne. I want someone on the ground at the office first thing tomorrow.'

'But what about the deal?'

'I'll handle the deal.'

'But…'

'Thank you, Adrian. That's all.'

Adrian turned, but not before he'd shot Mackenzi a look that told her he held her personally responsible for his slide from grace.

She shivered, both with the after effects of the let-down and from Adrian's frosty look. 'I get the distinct impression Adrian's less than impressed with your suggestion that I could help you with a project or two.'

He cast a glance in the direction of his deputy, who was sulkily scratching something into his PDA. 'I'm none to impressed with Adrian's advice lately. He can go and nurse his wounded pride back at the office. Meanwhile, we're staying in Auckland for the next few days while the architects and lawyers nut out the details. We're going to take a look at Quinn's outfit tomorrow, then check out the competition. It's going to be a busy few days, with more meetings and business dinners than you can imagine—you up to it?'

She smiled, feeling that strange, slow roll of her insides once more. She was not sure whether it was because he'd included her in that 'we're', or because it felt like today they'd turned some kind of corner where, despite their different goals, at least they'd proved they could work together.

And, even better, at least she'd be out there doing something with him and not stuck in the hotel waiting for him, wondering when, if ever, he was going to come back.

If they could work together, if she could show she could perform in the boardroom and not just the bedroom, wouldn't that give her more leverage when it came to changing his mind about Ashton House? So she'd bide her time, bite her tongue and wait for the perfect opportunity to raise the topic again.

'I'm looking forward to it,' she said.

* * *

Late the next day, Mackenzi felt like her head was going to explode. They'd done a tour of the site, checking out Quinn's existing facilities, had gone with Quinn to visit what felt like at least a dozen other boatyards, and now Quinn was driving them back to the hotel. Her head was bursting with facts and figures and new found nautical knowledge.

But her education hadn't finished there. She'd followed in Dante's wake today, marvelling at the speed with which he picked up new concepts and terminology and ran with them, gaining a new respect for a man whose fortune, she assumed, had been built solely by riding roughshod over anyone and everything.

But this was a new Dante. Even now, as talk in the car turned to the specifications of the new boatyard, it was easy to see that a new rapport had been established between the two men as they enthusiastically exchanged ideas, both of them united in wanting to move the proposal beyond concept stage and into reality as quickly as possible.

No wonder he was so successful at business, she reflected, when he immersed himself so completely in the world he was entering. He couldn't help but stay a step ahead of the competition.

She stole a glance at him while he spoke, feeling his enthusiasm, loving the energy that radiated out from him, the spark in the air around him. He turned, and caught her gaze and smiled at her through his words before turning his attention back to Quinn. It was only a moment, only a second that he'd turned her way, but Mackenzi felt the impact of his smile like a tripping of her thermostat, setting her blood to sizzle and her heartrate to overdrive.

Today she'd seen a different side to that ruthless businessman who had strong-armed his way into her life, and extracted a deal the devil himself would have been proud of.

A different side she wasn't entirely sure she was comfortable with.

It had been easier when she'd hated him. It had been easier when she'd had no respect for him. And it had been so much easier when a mere look had felt like damnation and not temptation.

For that was what he'd become…

They said goodbye to Quinn at the hotel, and Dante took her arm, his fingers like a brand to her flesh. Their eyes met briefly and she caught a glimmer of something simmering beneath the surface, hot and urgent, and finding an answering call in the tremor that moved her body onto high alert.

Without either of them uttering a word, there was no doubt at all in her mind what they'd be doing five minutes from now. This man had an appetite for sex that astounded her, an appetite that was as contagious as it was addictive. Already she could feel her need blossom in the dragging heat between her thighs and in the quickening of her breathing as her body prepared for the inevitable.

He guided her purposefully through the lobby towards the private lift that would take them to their penthouse suite. A man on a mission. *A man and his mistress.*

'It was a good day,' Dante said, his voice as tight as a drum, breaking his silence as he followed her into the lift.

'It was.'

The lift doors slid closed and he moved so quickly she didn't see him coming. In a heartbeat she felt herself pressed to the back of the lift, his hands working on her hungrily, hiking up her skirt, freeing himself in a rampaging, desperate rush. 'And it's about to get,' he added as he slid his long, hard length into her, 'one hell of a lot better.'

There were definitely worst fates than being someone's mistress, she decided as the lift doors opened and released them to their floor, dishevelled and windblown and bearing all the hallmarks of great sex.

'I'll run a bath,' she said, knowing Dante would want time to check his email.

He pulled her to him and kissed her hard on the lips. 'Thanks for the entrée. I'll be right there for the main course.'

She could barely stop smiling as she crossed the room on knees still shaky from their elevator encounter. There were definitely worse things than being Dante Carrazzo's mistress, that was for sure.

She stopped dead when she reached their bedroom. There were clothes spread out all over the bed and a rack of clothes parked nearby—sparkling evening gowns, linen suits and gorgeous day-dresses. Shoe boxes cluttered up the floor, and wide, flat boxes lined with tissue paper spilled over with underwear and accessories.

'Dante?' she called. 'What's all this?'

He came when she called and looked over her shoulder, his frown turning into a smile. 'Good, they've come.'

'You ordered them? What for?'

'You need more clothes,' Dante declared simply. 'It was no trouble to have the boutique send up a selection.'

The boutique downstairs; Mackenzi thought some of the clothes had looked familiar. Likewise she had no trouble remembering their price tags.

'I really think I can manage with what I've got.'

'Out of a suitcase the size of a shoe box? I don't think

so. I saw you this morning trying to recycle your wardrobe into something fresh and interesting. This solves all your problems. They've sent up your size. Just choose what you want and send the rest back.'

He kissed her on the cheek and made a move to go, as if already bored with the topic and satisfied she would happily comply, good little mistress that she was.

'But I don't want any of them,' she announced. 'For a start, their prices downstairs are ridiculous.'

He turned back. 'No-one said I was expecting you to pay for it. Anything you keep will be charged to the room.'

She shook her head. 'Oh no. You are not buying me clothes. I thought I'd made that clear.'

He took a step closer and raised one eyebrow high. 'You made it more than clear that you objected to being given jewellery. This isn't jewellery.'

She felt the euphoria of their love-making in the lift slide away, leaving her shaky and weak and all too well reminded that their encounter had had nothing to do with *who* she was and had been all about *what* she was.

And she'd thought there could be worse things than being Dante's mistress.

Not if being his mistress simultaneously made her his whore.

'I don't want the jewellery or the clothes, or anything. I don't want the trappings. I'm not that kind of mistress.'

'No? And I always thought mistress was a "one size fits all" concept. So *what* kind of mistress are you?'

She swallowed, her throat tight. 'You know I wouldn't be here unless you'd blackmailed me into it.'

His eyes turned cold and hard, his mouth curled into a malicious smile. 'Ah, the blackmailed mistress. As opposed to the mercenary mistress, I suppose? Is that how you see yourself?' He studied her face mercilessly, as if seeking any sign of weakness he could exploit. 'Or is it the altruistic mistress you fancy yourself as? The selfless virgin, sacrificing herself in order to save a crusty old pile of bricks?' He nodded, smiling wider as if pleased with his own analysis. 'Yes, I do believe it's the latter. Not that I recall any virgins.'

'Does it matter?' she argued, hating that he was laughing at her, and afraid his interpretation was too close to the mark. More afraid that anything she enjoyed so much could hardly be considered a sacrifice. 'I didn't agree to this deal for the trappings. I agreed to sleep with you, sure, and that's one thing I already have to work out how to come to terms with. But don't make it worse. Don't pay me for the privilege. Don't turn me into the whore you thought you'd found in your bed.'

Her voice broke on the final word and she spun around, her teeth clamping down hard on her bottom lip, her arms clenched tight around herself while tears stung at her eyes, pressing to be released.

Strong hands clasped her shoulders and she felt herself drawn back against the warmth of his body. 'I don't think that.' And when she tried to jerk away in protest he pulled her back against him. 'Not any more. Not now.'

'Then don't buy me things. It's enough that I'm here, sharing a suite that must be costing a fortune.'

He sighed, and pressed his lips to her ear. 'But you're practically part of the team now, working for me on this deal, and you need clothes. You know I'm right.'

'I won't wear clothes paid for by you and selected for me by some stick-insect shop assistant.'

He spun her around, and this time his smile looked genuine. 'Fine. Then go and choose them yourself. But, at the risk of offending you, I should mention that I intend paying for them—'

He hushed her rapid-fire protest with one touch of his lips on hers, a touch that melted her bones and brought her even closer. 'Let me finish,' he said, when at last he pulled his mouth away. 'I intend paying for them, out of the fee for your time and expertise while you assist me on this deal and any other for which I employ your services. A fee we will jointly negotiate, okay?'

She looked up into his eyes and almost wished she hadn't. After a kiss like that, a person could lose themselves in those eyes, could forget what they were arguing for. 'Okay,' she said at last. 'We'll talk about it.'

He hugged her tight and kissed her through his smile. 'Now, then, how about that spa? We've got some negotiating to do.'

CHAPTER TEN

IT HAD BEEN a productive week. Dante put the finishing touches to some notes he was preparing to email to his PA back in Melbourne and hit send. He leaned back in his chair and stretched his arms up high behind his head. It was Friday evening; Mackenzi was out shopping with Christine, finally having conceded that her inadequate wardrobe wasn't up to the task. The redesigned Quinn development was passing all kinds of tests—architectural, financial and otherwise—with the preliminary advice from the department responsible for zoning looking amenable to the development. But, if the days had been good, the nights had been better.

He was amazed that someone he'd selected as his 'deal or no deal' mistress could be so business-savvy. He was more amazed that his mistress, chosen on a whim after one insufficient night, had proved so bedroom-savvy.

He'd always loved the cut and thrust of business: the chase, the hunt, the satisfaction of achieving his goals. Women had always been ancillary to all of that—the answer to a need, the means to an end—and then they were gone.

But no longer. Now, after hours of sitting around in

boardrooms and offices, he couldn't wait to get Mackenzi back to their suite. Once he'd no sooner closed the door to their suite before he'd taken her up against it. Then there was the time he hadn't even waited that long, taking her in the lift the second the doors had slid closed.

But the best had been the slow times, like when they'd shared a bubble-filled spa and Mackenzi had been all slippery limbs, satiny skin and deliciously moist, inside and out. He'd slowly washed her all over, and she'd returned the compliment, her oiled hands working magic on his skin, turning mere flesh to steel. Finally, when they hadn't been able to take it any more, he'd lowered her down onto his lap until her hot, honeyed flesh had enveloped him, a languid start had become a frantic dash to the finish, and they'd both come in a heated rush that left them both gasping.

Just thinking about it made him hard again.

An email lobbed into his inbox and he glanced down at the screen, half-wishing he'd already closed down. He frowned when he saw it was from Adrian, his frown deepening when he registered the subject line: 'Ashton House Closure Date.' He clicked it open, marvelling how just the mention of that place could send his blood-pressure soaring and his mind to dark deeds.

Ashton House reservations had been approached, Adrian wrote, by a tour company that wanted to book tours, including Ashton House, in their itinerary for three successive years; they were awaiting advice whether they should accept.

Dante hadn't given a thought to Ashton House for days, but right now he stared at the email, feeling the familiar resentment build, the familiar clamp around his gut. It was always there, it seemed, simmering just below the surface, rancid and foul, waiting for an opportunity to boil over into his life. Right now he greeted the feeling like an old friend.

It was probably time he made some kind of decision. What was the point of putting it off? He'd made a deal with Mackenzi to think about it, and at least she couldn't accuse him of not holding up his part of the bargain.

He hit reply and typed three succinct words—'tell them no'—sending the message and closing down his computer before anything else he might need to respond to arrived.

He stood and strolled over to the windows, looking out over the impressive Auckland city-skyline under a cloud-filled sky, looking for a distraction. The police car tearing along the street below, its lights flashing, didn't do it for long. He looked at his watch, wondering how long it would be until Mackenzi made it back from her shopping expedition with Christine; Christine had been only too happy to take Mackenzi under her wing and show her *the* places to shop in Auckland. They'd been gone for hours. Which meant she had to be back soon.

Dante smiled as he headed for the bathroom, grateful to have a plan. Mackenzi would be tired after all that shopping. What better way to unwind than a nice relaxing spa?

Mackenzi studied the steady rise and fall of his chest while he slept, which for once seemed to coincide with it being dark outside. Dante was a hard task-master, his energy boundless, his drive phenomenal, and when finally he slept it was like he'd entered the sleep of the dead.

Weariness dragged at her too. It had been a frantic ten

days, working alongside him, and she felt like she'd been involved in a property-investment masterclass.

But the deal was looking more and more solid, the new plans featuring a state-of-the-art boat-building facility, a marina, a shopping plaza and restaurant precinct, as well as accommodation looking out over it all to the glorious harbour beyond. It was a thrill to know she was part of making it happen.

Just like it was a thrill to find herself in Dante's bed every night.

She rolled over onto her back and stared up at the darkened ceiling, remembering how good he'd made her feel tonight. He'd whisked her into his arms barely a moment after she'd entered their suite, ignoring the scatter of shopping bags and boxes, and already working his way under her clothes before they'd made it to the bedroom.

His passion had blown her away, from their first impossibly quick encounter on the bed tonight to the slow second-act in the spa. The danger of it was that he was seducing her mind in a way she'd never imagined. Oh, she'd known from that very first night that he was capable of a form of seduction she'd never experienced before, but she'd never realized how such a seduction could weaken one's own defences.

She felt a twinge low down in her belly and smiled with relief. *Any day now.* She'd been right not to bother Dante with her concerns about forgetting to take those pills, although it had been blind fear as to his reaction that had motivated her. But knowing it would have cast a cloud over the last few days—and nights—and they'd both brought enough baggage into this relationship already. Besides which, there was no point both of them worrying.

But, as much as she found herself enjoying the love-making aspect of being Dante's mistress much more than she'd expected, she knew she couldn't let this bedroom bargain drag on forever. A week or two, he'd estimated their affair would last. It was already more than that and still there were no signs of him wearying of her. Surely that meant something? Surely after all they'd shared together, after all the passionate highs and more they'd shared, Dante must feel something for her? She'd sensed something in his declaration that he didn't consider her his whore, and she wanted to believe it, even if what he felt for her was only a little respect. That would be enough. Surely he would listen to her now?

So maybe it was time. She hadn't mentioned Ashton House since that day out on the boat. Maybe it was time to test the waters and raise the subject again.

The next few days passed in a blur. Instead of a quiet weekend in Auckland like she'd been expecting after their hectic week, Dante announced early the next morning that they were flying down to Wellington to check out several properties he'd listed to inspect. So they spent the weekend in the company of property agents, touring shopping complexes thronging with shoppers, and visiting office-towers strangely hushed and empty. Once, when they had a couple of hours to themselves and they'd walked down to the harbour, Dante stopped to buy ice creams. They strolled hand-in-hand along the shore of Oriental Bay, surrounded by joggers and families out cycling and other couples holding hands, the fresh breeze whipping around them, tugging at their hair and jackets.

He was so warm, so unusually conversational, talking with her about the distinctive architecture of the properties lining the bay, about their colour and character. He'd never looked more approachable and Mackenzi almost raised the subject of Ashton House then. Until he told her she had chocolate on her lip, and he held back the hand that was on its way to wipe it, dipping his head down to kiss it off, the touch of his tongue against her lip electric; something tiny, tender and fragile had burst into life inside her.

They could have been any other couple walking the bay that day, and anyone else would have believed they were just a normal couple in love. The moment was so tender and sweet, and the risks that she would spoil this fragile sense of camaraderie between them too great, that she chose to say nothing.

The nights were too precious, their love-making so passionate, exquisite and explosive, never failing to rock her world and deliver her, fully sated, into the arms of sleep.

And before she knew it they were back in Auckland and he'd whisked her off on a launch to visit Waiheke Island and inspect more property. This time it was residential, although the properties he showed her looked more like palaces than every-day houses, with their sprawling, tropical gardens complete with tennis courts and swimming pools, and the all-too-necessary helipad for the daily commute to the city.

Then it was back to the endless round of meetings and dinners with architects, financiers and lawyers and there was no time to think of anything but the matters at hand.

Until it occurred to her. The twinges and cramps that had started out so promisingly had faded away to nothing.

She was four days late.

CHAPTER ELEVEN

MACKENZI STARED down at the bold blue line and knew her life had changed forever.

Because she was no longer just late.

She was pregnant.

Fear jagged through her like the slash of a bread knife, throwing her off balance, so that she had to grab hold of the marble bathroom vanity just to keep herself upright. Dante's bedroom bargain had just got a whole lot more complicated.

It wasn't just bad enough that she was pregnant. She was pregnant with Dante Carrazzo's child. And somehow she would have to find a way to tell him.

Now she couldn't put off talking to him. Now there could be no waiting for the right moment, no giving way to the worry that she might spoil something precious. Because everything was ruined. She was pregnant to Dante Carrazzo. And things couldn't possibly get any worse.

She stared at her reflection in the mirror, looking for changes, seeking any telltale sign that she should have noticed, something that could have alerted her to the possibility that she was pregnant. But her nose looked as asymmetrical as it ever had, and her eyes blinked back at her as green as ever, maybe just a little jaded. But she was bound to be tired, surely, with the hectic pace Dante kept up day and night?

God, a baby. What the hell was she going to do with a baby? How would she cope, a single mother trying to work the crazy hours of a job in the hospitality industry? Assuming she could get a job when she got home. Applying, pregnant and single, for a senior position like she'd held before was not going to win her any favours.

What the hell was she going to do?

She took a couple of deep breaths. First things first. She'd need to see a doctor and have her discovery confirmed. There was no point saying anything about it until then, because it could be a false positive, couldn't it? Her weary eyes looked back at her. *Fat chance*, they said.

Dante called from outside, interrupting her thoughts and letting her know their breakfast had arrived. Her stomach instantly rebelled at the prospect of food. Or was it just at his voice, knowing what lay in store for her? If the doctor did confirm the worst then she knew she was going to have to tell him. She just wished she knew how she was going to do it.

Mackenzi turned on the shower she should have finished five minutes ago and let the water cascade over her, vacantly soaping herself, one hand unconsciously coming to rest over the place underneath where a brand-new life was taking shape. What kind of mother would she be? Her own parents had struggled for years to have a child, finally resorting to technology in a bid to achieve their dream. She had known she was wanted, and desperately so, for her entire life. She had been loved. Was loved.

And yet here she was, pregnant through misadventure. Through an act of carelessness, if she wanted to be honest. Did that mean she would love her child any less? *Please God, no.*

And how would Dante take to fatherhood? She had no way of knowing, no hint as to his background, upbringing or family life. All she did know was that he was passionate and driven, and yet he could be tender, could be so achingly tender. But there was an ugly side to Dante, something twisted and bitter, something that turned him into an agent of destruction.

Steam fogged the room, turning the air thick and way too sultry. One thing, though, was crystal clear: a child of hers deserved better than a father who was hell-bent on destruction. Any decision Dante made on the future of Ashton House was going to determine how much he had to do with his baby's life.

Maybe he'd surprise her. Maybe that tenderness he'd displayed to her of late meant something more than mere respect. And maybe there was a chance, if he could relent on the fate of the hotel, that they might be able to work out a way to share custody of the child.

But, if he was going to go ahead with his plans to destroy the hotel and the building, she'd make sure his child had as little to do with its father as possible.

In her heart of hearts she dearly wished it wouldn't come to that.

She snapped off the shower and dried quickly, wrapping herself in her robe. She hid the stick and packaging in her toiletries bag and let herself out of the bathroom, feeling shaky and breathless with the aftershock of her discovery, her mind almost overcome from trying to unravel the sudden tangle her life had become.

Dante was seated at the table, poring over the business pages. 'You took your time,' he said without looking up. He'd poured her coffee and for the first time ever the smell of the dark, rich roast he preferred threatened to turn her stomach. She clamped down on the feeling, pushing the cup away.

'Dante, we need to talk.'

'That sounds ominous,' he said in a voice that sounded like he was expecting to hear news that was anything but. He picked up his cup and took a long sip of the steaming black fluid, and looked up at her, his brow puckering when he saw her face.

She turned her face away. Now she couldn't even bear to look at a cup of coffee. What was happening to her? She heard the sound of his cup meeting the saucer. 'What's on your mind?'

Too much to think straight. 'A couple of things.'

'Spit them out, then.' He already sounded impatient.

Her head bowed, she turned her eyes up towards him. 'You know the deal we made, the promise you made to me to reconsider your decision to close Ashton House?'

She had his full attention now. She could see it in the hardening of his eyes, the firming of his jaw and the body language that turned his shoulders and chest warrior-like.

'Do we have to discuss this now? We have a meeting with Quinn in an hour.'

'Dante, this is important. It can't wait any longer.'

He ground his jaw. 'What about our deal?'

She took a deep breath. 'Well, you thought this arrangement would last a week, maybe two…'

'And?'

'And it's been that and longer! I've been your mistress, I've slept in your bed. I've kept up my end of the deal.'

'I haven't noticed you complaining.'

'I'm not complaining. It's just that I'm not sure I can do this any more.'

'So you're calling the deal off?'

'No! I just need to know where you stand. You promised me you'd think about your decision to destroy Ashton House. I've kept up my end of the bargain. Have you?'

His eyes glared back at her, glazed and frosty. A muscle in his jaw popped. 'I've thought about it, yes.'

As if she'd picked up the temperature from his eyes, her blood ran ice-cold with foreboding.

'And?'

'My decision stands.'

She stood, her body unable to take the shock of his announcement sitting down, every part of her at war with his words. 'What? You can't mean that, not after everything that's happened. You're actually going to go ahead and close Ashton House?'

'That's my decision.'

'But you can't do that. Not now—'

'The decision has been made.'

'When was it made? You didn't tell me you'd already decided. You let me go on thinking…'

'You unexpectedly proved quite useful in business, and

were a very pleasant diversion after hours. Why shorten the affair unnecessarily?'

His callous assessment of her worth was like a body blow. '"Useful in business"? Aren't you forgetting that I saved your deal? Without me you wouldn't have one.'

'And I tried to thank you and you threw your gift back in my face!'

Blood hammered in her ears, the drumbeat of fury and turmoil and utter devastation as something fragile and hopeful inside her crumpled, leaving only anger in its wake. 'I don't believe you even thought about it. I think you had your mind made up from day one and you were never going to change it!'

He stood, tossing the unfinished newspaper aside. 'You can believe what you like. But that was a risk you took when you agreed to this deal.'

'But if you'd thought about it you'd see how utterly insane it is. That there's no point—'

'The matter is closed. I take it that means our arrangement is at an end?'

His ice-cold rapier words sliced through her, but it was the question contained in them that incensed her more than anything.

'How can you possibly imagine I'd want to stay now?'

A shadow moved across his eyes, something fleeting and unreadable. 'A shame, though. It was good while it lasted.'

She gulped. 'If you say so.'

His eyes turned to a glare. 'I'll let Quinn know to tell Christine you've had to fly back suddenly to Adelaide.' He tossed her a card from his wallet. 'Adrian will take care of your travel arrangements.'

She tore the card in pieces and let them scatter where they fell. 'He damn well won't! I'm quite capable of making my own flight bookings.'

He stood there, as hard as a statue, the barely restrained fury emanating out from him not in a heated rage but in a cold, dank aura. Then he reached up on a breath and straightened his tie. 'So be it. I want you packed and gone when I get back.'

Mackenzi stood watching him, unable to believe what had just happened as he strode to the office to organize his briefcase. So it had come to this? She'd outlived her use-by date and now it was time for him to discard her. Even though she'd always known it *could* end this way—had from the very first day realized that she'd been kidding herself and that he'd been using her, determined never to change his mind—she'd never expected the gut-wrenching agony that accompanied her worst fears coming true.

Where had the tender Dante gone, the man who'd kissed ice cream from her lips and kindled the faint hope of something worthwhile in her heart? Now, where once there'd been hope, there was only grief.

Because she'd not only lost the hotel.

Her baby had lost its father.

Forever.

'I thought you'd changed,' she said to his broad, resolute back as he shoved papers and spreadsheets and plans into his briefcase. 'I thought you'd learned something with the Quinn contract—that you don't have to destroy things, that there's worth in building instead.'

'Ashton House is different.'

'You've said that before. Why is it different?'

'It just is!'

'But look at what you're doing. You're not just destroy-ing a building and a heritage, you're messing with peoples' lives, the people who work there, the people who were married there and who love the old place, like my parents and half the rest of the local community.'

He threw her a look that came with an acid burn, like he didn't want to hear it, like he didn't want to know. Too bad. He was going to hear it anyway. He *deserved* to hear it!

'And what do you think it's going to do to the former owners, Jonas and Sara Douglas, when they learn what you have planned for Ashton House? They were devastated merely to lose control of the property. What do you think it will do to them to see their pride and joy lie in ruins?'

He turned towards her then, his eyes like black holes, his features desolate. 'Destroy them, I hope.'

Shock transfixed her, his voice so bleak, his expression so nightmarish and his words like a curse.

Which was the real Dante, she wondered—the passion-ate lover with a streak so tender it brought tears to her eyes, or this tormented creature, little more than an animal in pain?

'What happened to you?' she asked, putting voice to the questions in her mind, 'To turn you into such a monster?'

The way his lips curled into what she took to be a smile almost sickened her. 'You think I'm a monster?'

'How else would you describe what you have planned? Especially when the Douglases have already had such a tragic life.'

'Tragic? Jonas gambled his fortune away. What's tragic about that?'

'And who could blame him? They'd lost both their sons!

What parent would survive that intact? And now they've seen their property fortune whittled away bit by bit. They're going to be left with practically nothing. And why? What have they ever done to you?'

He laughed then, if it could have been called that, and she winced at the sound, discordant, like nails scraping on a blackboard. 'It's more than they ever left me.'

A premonition of something dark and fetid rolled through her, and she shuddered, torn between wanting to know and fearful for what he might say. 'What do you mean?' she whispered. 'More than they ever left you?'

He clicked his briefcase shut and the sound seemed to rouse him. 'I have a meeting to go to. Let yourself out.'

'Dante! No.' She met him at the door, reaching out a hand to his arm to stop him. She couldn't let him go, not like this, not when he was so tortured. His anguish was so real and so raw that, in spite of every last hurtful thing he'd said to her today, her heart just wouldn't let him walk out of here. She cared too much to see him go this way.

And like a thunderbolt it hit her.

She'd fallen in love with Dante Carrazzo.

He looked down at her hand on his arm, then to her face, as if expecting her to say something, to plead, to beg, to remonstrate some more. But she was dumbstruck, rendered mute by the realization that, against all her best intentions, she'd fallen in love with a man who could be a monster. Silence hung between them, the quiet drone of the air conditioning unit the only sound.

He shrugged off her hand, pulled open the door and marched out of her life.

The lift descended like a stone, his gut along with it,

until when he reached the ground floor he felt he'd hit rock bottom.

Damn!

Why had she had to do that when everything had been going so well? Why had she had to ask? He was going to miss her input into his daily business dealings. He was going to miss her after hours even more.

Dante stepped out into the lobby, the taste of coffee stale in his mouth, the bitter finish to an unsatisfactory breakfast. The smell of rain met him, a gust of wind slamming into him as the lobby doors opened, releasing him into the grey outside world. Beyond the covered drive-through the rain-lashed city looked bleak and drab. Damn right.

He walked past the driver who'd been waiting for him, signalling that he wouldn't be needing him, shrugging away his proffered umbrella. It was the perfect day to walk.

Why had she had to ask? She hadn't seemed unhappy the last few days, quite the reverse. Lately she'd been less like a mistress and more like an extension of himself, a part of him. He'd got used to having her around. What had prompted her to do it? *Stupid.*

In the street the wind-driven rain struck his face, needle sharp and icy cold. It should hurt, he registered somewhere through the fog in his mind. It should at least sting. But he felt nothing, nothing but the anger. A different anger, he recognized, or at least a different flavour of the anger.

He'd felt the familiar heat rising at her mention of Ashton House, but somehow the edge had been missing, that almost quintessential hatred, the pinnacle of loathing. He'd had to fight to find it, had had to fight *her* to feed his need.

And, to Mackenzi's credit, she'd not failed him. She'd

defended Ashton House with that undying loyalty she'd shown from day one, but her real *pièce de résistance* had been in beseeching him to care about what happened to Jonas and Sara Douglas.

Oh, he cared all right, but not in the way she wanted. He cared so much he'd see them rot in hell, even if it meant he'd be rotting right there alongside them, it would be worth it.

The rain grew heavier, pedestrians fleeing for cover, their umbrellas turned inside out, car headlights fighting the gloom and making crazy patterns on the slick road, and still he walked on. Uncaring. Unfeeling.

Mackenzi had tightened the screws and had found the one thing that could turn his anger incendiary.

So why did he feel so bad? Why did it taste different? Inside him his gut still felt as solid as a stone, like a cannon ball set loose, weighing him down. Rain streaked down his face, running trails past his collar down his neck and beyond, until he could feel the wet patches soaking into his shirt, his coat no protection against the remorseless weather. His shoes hit a puddle and filled with water, squelching between his toes.

It should feel cold. The thought came from nowhere, yet somewhere, deep in the jumbled fog of his mind. He should feel something. Instead he just felt empty.

He remembered her face then, her upturned face as she'd tried to stop him. He'd thought she was going to say something, but her parted lips had halted halfway to a word and she'd looked up at him with something akin to terror in her eyes.

It had frightened the hell out of him.

He'd done that to her. He'd used her like a punching bag to feed his own desperate need.

Mackenzi deserved better.

He stopped at traffic lights, waiting for the green light to cross, and still the rain came down, the truth of his thoughts finally sinking in. She didn't deserve it—not to be treated like that. One day she would have had to find out about his plans for the hotel, that he could never change them. Maybe he might have even told her why. Not that anyone else would understand.

But he hadn't had to do it that way. He hadn't had to hurt her. And he was sure he had.

He remembered her face and that expression. The terror. The fear.

God, what had he done?

The lights changed, the green 'walk' signal lighting up at last, and Dante started to walk.

He let himself into the suite, peeled off his drenched topcoat and dropped his briefcase, aware but uncaring that he was trailing a puddle of water with every step. She wasn't in the dining room, the plates still scattered on the table where he'd left them, her coffee untouched. The bedroom bore signs of frantic activity, clothes thrown into a suitcase, but the open wardrobe still full of the clothes she'd bought here.

He found her in the bathroom, sitting on the edge of the bath and still in the robe. Her hair was a mess and she was blowing her nose, looking down at something in her other hand.

She looked up suddenly, and the cannon ball inside him

careened wildly when he saw her eyes were red and puffy, like she'd been crying.

'Dante! You're back.' She frowned, her hand whipping whatever it was she was holding out of sight. 'What happened to you?'

But right now he was more interested in what she was hiding than answering her question, his reason for coming back already forgotten. 'What the hell is that?'

CHAPTER TWELVE

'I WAS…I was just packing,' she said, standing now, still hiding whatever it was she had hidden now under her robe. Mackenzi made a play of picking up things from the counter and sticking them in her toiletries bag, but he swiped up the box and the unfolded sheet of print lying nearby, her frantic rescue actions too late to save them.

'What is this?' he said as the description on the box confirmed all his worst fears, the box now containing only one of the two tests listed in the contents. He looked at her. 'What the hell are you doing with a pregnancy kit?'

Fight returned to her red-rimmed eyes and the set of her chin. 'I was going to change the washers with it. What do you think I'm doing with it?'

'Show me what's in your hand.'

'Why? It's none of your business. You've already terminated my services. Again.'

'Show me!'

She sniffed, her eyes now looking more uncertain, a quiver in her bottom lip betraying how close she must be again to tears as her hand reluctantly withdrew from under her robe. Shakily she held the test out towards him and he took it. The cannon ball in his gut grew larger until there was no room for even the air in his lungs.

'Satisfied? That line means a negative result.' But her voice sounded less than convincing, and the information on the box in bold print also contradicted what she was saying. He looked at her, not knowing what he felt except that something was terribly, terribly wrong.

'You're pregnant.'

Her face crumpled on a groan and she collapsed down onto the side of the bath once more, this time with her head in her hands. 'Yes.'

The question that had been grating on his nerves ever since the possibility she was pregnant had entered his mind just had to be asked. 'So whose baby is it?'

Her head snapped back up. 'Whose baby do you think it is?'

'You tell me. You're the woman I found lying in wait for me in my bed. How do I know how many other beds you've taken to in your quest to get whatever you want?'

She turned and looked at him. 'I wasn't lying in wait for you that night, Dante. I was sleeping over in an empty bed because I'd worked late and had an early start the next morning. Nothing more.'

He shook his head, discounting her claims. If that was the truth then none of this would have happened, she would have run from his bed kicking and screaming. 'What about your friend Richard?'

She laughed. Or it could have been a sob; he wasn't sure. 'Ancient history.'

'But more likely than me. I've known you, what, three

weeks? This thing doesn't tell me how long you've been pregnant. How do I know it's not months?'

She raised herself to as much height as she could muster in her bare feet and glared at him. 'It's *your* baby, Dante. A scan will soon confirm any dates, and if you need more a blood test later will give you all the proof you need. You're the *father*, God help the poor child.' And then she collected her toilet bag and pushed past him through the bedroom and into the living room.

He stood for a while as his mind grappled with the unfamiliar concept that someone might be carrying a child of his. From the vehemence of his words there emerged the tiny seed of possibility that it might be true—that it *was* true—and that seed gave birth to the idea that somehow this might even be a good thing. Mackenzi, pregnant with his child.

Not that it made any sense.

He tracked her movements across the floor, not understanding, finding her standing by the windows, her robe tightly tied at her waist and her arms crossed while her hair tumbled down her back in a riot of disarray. My God, he thought, even like this without a skerrick of make-up to mask her reddened eyes she was still beautiful. But still he didn't understand. 'You told me you were on the Pill.'

One hand came out beseechingly, her elbow still locked at her waist. 'I was! I mean, I am, but I missed one…or two.'

'How the hell did that happen?'

She screwed up her face, remembering. 'That night I stayed at the hotel. I slept over some nights in the hotel when I was working late, but I'd taken my overnight bag out of my car and I'd left my pills at home. I missed one. I didn't think it would matter, but then we left so quickly for Auckland that I forgot about it until the day after we arrived…'

'Don't give me that! You were lying there in wait for me the whole time and you can't pretend you weren't—not with the reception you gave me. And yet you still *forgot* to take two pills in a row? How careless was that?'

She abandoned any hope of convincing him she hadn't been lying in wait for him that night and gestured instead towards the bedroom. 'About as careless, I guess, as you forgetting to use protection when you jammed me up and took me against that wall in there. The same way you neglected to use a condom when you made love to me in the lift between floors three and twenty-three. People forget things, Dante, even you apparently!'

'You should have told me.'

'Would you have wanted me to tell you something like that? I don't think so.'

Something in her words stuck in his craw. 'You weren't going to tell me about the baby either, were you? You were going to walk out of here without telling me.'

'You told me you wanted me gone. I was only too happy to oblige.'

'But you knew then, didn't you? You knew you were pregnant. That's what all that talk about our deal was about, wasn't it?'

'I wanted to know where I stood. You made that more than plain.'

'But you didn't tell me!'

'And you didn't deserve to know!'

He wheeled away. He'd been an utter bastard to her this morning, he knew it. But she'd known she was having his child and yet she hadn't said a word, had kept the truth from him. She was no innocent herself!

'So what are you planning to do?'

She gave a defeated shrug of her shoulders. 'I don't know. Go home. Get a job.'

'How can you work?'

'I'm not sick, Dante, just pregnant, and only just. And it's early days, who knows what might happen?'

'You will not have an abortion!'

'I meant that nature might take its course and decide that for itself.'

'And what will you do after the child is born? How will you cope with a child and a job?'

'I don't know. But I will. And if worst comes to worst I guess there's always the adoption route.'

'No child of mine will be adopted out!'

The force of his reply took her by surprise. She hadn't meant it, she'd been doing no more than thinking out loud, couldn't he see that?

'And who are you, telling me what to do?'

'I won't let you give this baby up!'

'So now you care what I do when you practically threw me out this morning?'

'I didn't know then that you might be carrying my child.'

'*Am* carrying your child,' she corrected. 'But believe what you like. I need to finish my packing. Meanwhile—' she looked pointedly at the clock '—didn't you have a meeting to attend? You might want to shower and change first, though, right now you look like something the cat dragged in.'

He growled and glanced at the time. Damn the meeting!

This was more important. 'You're not going anywhere,' he ordered. 'And you're certainly not flying, not until we've had you properly checked out.'

'Forget it, Dante. I've had enough. I'm leaving, and you can't stop me.' She set off for the bedroom and he made a move to follow her when the phone rang, loud and insistent, and he knew they would be looking for him. But he had a job to do here, he had to keep Mackenzi from leaving, and he couldn't trust her to stay if he wasn't here.

The phone stopped ringing and when he got to the bedroom he saw why. Mackenzi looked at him, handset to ear. 'Sorry, Stuart, I'm feeling off-colour and won't make the meeting, but Dante's just on his way.'

He fired his toughest glare at her as he pulled the handset out of her hand. 'Quinn! Sorry to keep you waiting. We've had a bit of a crisis here this morning, but it's all sorted out now.'

Mackenzi shot him daggers from across the room as she collected up the last of her paltry collection and dropped them in her case.

'No, the doctor will be here shortly. But that's not all that's held me up this morning. Did she tell you our good news?'

Mackenzi stopped dead and looked up at him in horror, suddenly shaking her head desperately. He smiled back at her as Quinn urged him to spill the news. 'It's very exciting news, actually. Mackenzi's just agreed to become my wife.'

'What the hell were you thinking? Why did you tell him that?' Mackenzi's mind still reeled with the fallout from his announcement, her thought processes already all but shredded with the turmoil and emotion of the morning.

He shrugged, a look of victory turning his face smug as he started unbuttoning his drenched shirt, rifling through the wardrobe with his free hand for another. 'It's the perfect solution,' he said. 'The baby will have a mother and a father, and you won't have to go out to work.'

'Aren't you forgetting something?'

He pulled the shirt over his head and dropped it on the carpet, where it landed with a dull slap. 'I don't think so.'

'You haven't asked me. And, even if you did, I'd say no. I won't marry you, Dante. I wouldn't marry you if you were the last man left on earth.'

He straightened then and she almost wished he hadn't, and for the very same reason she was glad he had. The muscles rippled under that broad, hard chest and drew her gaze and turned her thoughts to other times, to other more pleasurable activities. How was it that she'd ever believed she was frigid? She wrenched the tie around her waist tighter, pressing down on her own body's reaction, wishing she had dressed when he had gone this morning rather than dissolving into tears and thinking pointless 'what if?'s.

'You seemed to enjoy being my mistress well enough.'

'Marriage isn't just about enjoyment, though, is it? It's about love and respect and mutual desire to build something together. You're not into building anything are you, Dante? Except for your own personal fortune, and then only so you can tear someone else's down!'

He walked towards her, his torso a sculpture in motion, and she held her breath. She wanted a denial. She wanted him to say that he wanted to marry her for more than just the child they'd conceived between them. That he'd changed and that he'd come to love her, even just a little, and that he could learn to love her more over time. She wanted to know that her own newly discovered love was not in vain.

'It won't be a normal marriage,' he said, turning her hopes to dust. Then he took the fingers of one hand and traced them down her cheek and along the line of her jaw. She closed her eyes and swallowed as his touch set her senses on fire, her nipples budding and pressing against the towelling robe. 'But the experience we've already had together,' he continued, 'tells us it can be better than tolerable.'

Her breath hitched when his fingers ran down the slope of her neck, dipping further, transgressing the line between robe and flesh. She knew what they were telling her—that it would be worth marrying Dante for the sex alone. She almost believed them. *Almost.*

'No,' she said, gripping the neckline of her robe tightly together, another greater purpose occurring to her in a lightning bolt of inspiration. 'If I'm to marry you, there has to be something in it for me.'

His hand curled around her neck and pulled her closer to him so she was nestled against his body, the scent of fresh rain and naked skin teasing her nostrils. 'I'll be more than enough for you, you know that.'

'Maybe. But you get a child out of this marriage. I want something concrete too.'

He put his hands to her shoulders and pushed her away, watching her warily, his eyes narrowed. 'So, what is it you want?'

'For you to save Ashton House. Change your mind about destroying it and I'll marry you. Otherwise, no deal.'

He laughed and let her go. 'Sure. I promise to think about it.'

'No way,' she said. 'That's not how this deal works. The time for thinking is past. I want a cast-in-gold guarantee here. If I marry you, then Ashton House stays a going concern, and it never gets pulled down by you or any of your other cronies.'

'And if I don't agree?'

'Then not only will I refuse to marry you, I'll do my utmost to see you have as little as possible to do with your child.'

'You won't be able to stop me. Legally I can make you give me access.' He strode to the wardrobe, took hold of his new shirt and pulled it off the hanger.

'And why would you even want access? Unless you want to turn its mind toxic, so it ends up half-crazed just like its dear old dad?' She shook her head. 'No way. You're not doing that to my child. And you can argue with me all you want but you're going to have to fight me. Because there's no way I'm agreeing to this marriage without your guarantee not to destroy Ashton House first.'

'You expect me to agree to an ultimatum like that?'

'It's a simple choice,' she told him, feeling suddenly emboldened, her heart pumping fast in her chest. 'You can go on living in the past, or you can build a brand-new future of your own.'

Dante looked at her, his new shirt still in his hands, although the collar was starting to look mighty creased. She could see that for once she held the advantage, for once she had the upper hand, and she couldn't help but also notice that he knew it too and hated the fact.

'But you'll marry me, in spite of all my obvious

faults, of which there are clearly many, if I agree to save Ashton House?'

'As simple as that,' she said.

Mackenzi held her breath as he purposefully strode away, standing with hands on hips at the window, looking out over the cityscape below. She didn't expect a quick decision; she knew that Dante would sooner agree to give her the moon and wouldn't fail to come through with it. But as the time ticked by she started to wonder if she hadn't overplayed her hand. She knew how he felt about Ashton House, even though she would never understand his reasons why. How could an unplanned and unborn child, barely conceived, compete with Dante's passion for destruction?

Finally he turned around and looked over at her. Even from here she could see the throbbing pulse in the cords of his neck and light sheen of perspiration lining his brow, and she knew what her request must have cost him. Through clenched teeth he managed the words, 'I'll do it. It's a deal. But I have my conditions too.'

'Which are?'

'We'll do this wedding my way.' She opened her mouth to protest and he held up one hand to stall her. 'Listen first. We get married as soon as legally possible, I assume that's going to be at least four weeks. And I expect you'll want this marriage to take place at Ashton House?'

She nodded. She'd been going to request it. It would mean so much to her parents and to her, even though she'd known she would be really pushing it with Dante. 'If it's at all available. And it's not as if it had to be held on a weekend.'

'Fine. Then I'll have Adrian take care of all the details.'

'Adrian? But——'

'That's my condition. I don't want you worrying about details. You concentrate on finding yourself a dress. He can take care of everything else.'

'I think my mother might like some say in the arrangements,' she ventured, wanting at least some input into the process. 'Otherwise she'll think this is an even stranger wedding.'

'All right. I'll make sure he liaises with your mother. Anything else?'

She blinked, her mind trying to catch up, stunned by the speed at which her bold challenge was fast becoming a reality. Her blood fizzed in the excitement of knowing how close she was to achieving her goal when all had looked lost—to saving Ashton House.

But there was another more selfish layer to her excitement than that. It was the certain knowledge that within a few weeks she would be wife to the man she secretly loved, when she became Mrs Dante Carrazzo.

She shook her head. 'That all sounds fine.'

'Then it's a deal.'

In the days and nights that followed she could have all too easily believed their impending marriage was for real. Dante took her to the exclusive jewellery store downstairs to select a ring, and the manager was more than happy to show them the best. Mackenzi had only wanted something small—to spend a lot under the circumstances seemed wrong—but Dante disagreed and insisted upon the best. The ring they finally settled upon was both bewitchingly simple and yet dazzling in its beauty. Mackenzi loved it.

The Quinns were delighted with the engagement news,

insisting on taking them out to celebrate, making sure the papers were on hand to photograph the happy couple.

And Mackenzi did feel happy, and apart from a bit of shakiness in the early mornings she had never felt better. Her pregnancy, still their own precious secret, was confirmed and shown as viable with an ultrasound scan that had taken her breath away. Dante sat alongside her, trying with her to make sense of the shadowed images, until finally the picture had become clear and they saw it together—the beating of their baby's tiny heart. He took her hand and squeezed it, and her own heart filled to bursting as together they stared at the miracle of new life they'd created together.

There was real hope for them, she decided right then and there. There was good in Dante, and they could build a future together based not just around a baby but grounded in love; she knew it.

The Quinn deal was ultimately wrapped up, another property they'd viewed in Wellington contracted, and Dante returned with Mackenzi to Melbourne, installing her in his Toorak mansion with strict instructions to do nothing more taxing than to shop for her wedding dress. He even surprised her by flying her mother over to help her.

He loves me, she told herself, trying on one more gown and looking at her reflection in the mirror as the dresser adjusted the spread of the short train behind her. He'd been so thoughtful, so considerate, lately and yet still he'd been the consummate lover in the bedroom, which had first brought them together that first night. *He must love me.*

The dresser took a moment longer to fix a short veil to complete the outfit then stood alongside her and nodded appreciatively at the picture in the mirror. Mackenzi smiled. The dress hugged her body like a glove, the cream-coloured silk perfectly complementing her skin and hair colouring, the design simple yet elegant.

'What do you think?' she asked her mother when she emerged from the dressing room a moment later. But she could read the answer in her mother's tear-filled eyes as she stood there, hands pressed together as though in prayer. 'You look so beautiful,' her mother cried. 'That's the one.'

Mackenzi did not have a shred of doubt that she was doing the right thing or that she was cheating her parents out of 'the real deal' with this rushed marriage. As far as she was concerned, this was the real deal, and she knew in her heart that they could make it work.

There was nothing surer.

CHAPTER THIRTEEN

THE WEDDING DAY dawned misty and damp, an early-morning shower leaving the air fresh and crisp, the clear sky bearing promise of a sun-kissed spring day. A perfect day for a garden wedding. Mackenzi stood on the balcony of her suite and breathed in the cool, clear air, relishing being back in the Adelaide Hills again, letting the classic atmosphere of Ashton House wrap its way around her. It was good to be home.

She'd spent the night alone, as tradition dictated, and already she was anticipating the thrill of spending tonight and every following night with Dante, this time as neither his mistress nor his fiancée, but as his wife.

Excitement fizzed in her veins, radiating out along her limbs until even her fingers and toes tingled. She hugged the feeling to herself. She was the luckiest woman alive.

The morning passed in a blur of appointments—hairdresser, manicurist and make-up artists all wanting a piece of her, her mother clucking around organizing things like a good mother should. Mackenzi loved every minute of it. She was still in her robe, preparing to put on her dress, her mother and bridesmaid in the midst of having their hair done, when there was a buzz at the door. One hairdresser made a move to answer it but Mackenzi put a hand up. 'I'll get it,' she said, as she was closest to the entry lobby. 'That should be the flowers.'

'Just make sure it's not Dante!' they called out in a chorus behind her. She laughed as she peered through the spy hole, her stomach dropping when she saw who it was.

Adrian. Holding a box of flowers. She hadn't seen him since that day he'd been ordered on the next flight out of Auckland. She hadn't been looking forward to seeing him again, but he had organised her wedding, and today of all days she couldn't be churlish.

She opened the door, forcing something of a smile to return, although the way his eyes narrowed as they scanned her from top to bottom told her his view of her hadn't improved any. She wished she had more than scanty underwear on under her robe.

'Your flowers have arrived,' he said tightly, holding out the box towards her.

'Thank you,' she said, giving them little more than a glance through the cellophane window. There would be time to admire them later. 'By the way, I haven't had a chance to thank you for everything you've done for me in organising this wedding.'

His mouth angled up as his lips pressed together. 'It was my job,' he said, as if he undertook such menial impositions every day whether he wanted to or not.

'Oh, well, thanks anyway.' She put out her hands to take the box and he made a subtle movement, tugging it away.

'I was surprised, quite frankly.'

'Oh?' she said, watching the box, wondering if she'd

merely imagined or misinterpreted what had just happened. 'What about?'

'To find you still hanging around.'

Now he had her full attention. 'What are you talking about?'

'Only that I thought you would have given up, now that your cause is lost.'

'What are you talking about?'

'The deal you had with Dante, to sleep with him in exchange for him thinking about the future of this fine establishment.'

The hackles at the back of her neck rose. Adrian knew the details of their deal? No wonder he looked at her as if she were soiled. But she wasn't about to take the dirt from him. 'But that's old news, Adrian, it isn't an issue any more. Ashton House is safe.'

'Is it, indeed?' His eyes grew malicious, his smirk more knowing. 'You mean he hasn't told you?'

Fear washed through her, threatening to buckle her knees, not wanting to hear more but needing to ask. 'Told me what?'

'That the hotel is closing.' He pressed the box into her hands and sneered. 'Enjoy your wedding.'

She turned and walked blindly back into the room, placing the flowers on the bed to the appreciative 'ooh's and 'aah's from the womenfolk. She left them to it and picked up the phone, Reception picking up a few rings later—*it couldn't be true*.

'Natalie?' she said, recognizing the girl and ignoring as tactfully as she could her questions as to how everything was going and how it was all so exciting. 'What's happening with the hotel? I heard a rumour it's closing?'

It's a lie, she told herself while she waited, her heart thumping so loud she was sure Natalie would be able to hear it. *It has to be a lie.*

'That's right,' said Natalie, and then with some trepidation, 'I thought you would have known—'

He'd lied to her! Mackenzi dropped the receiver in a clatter, turning, not bothering to check if it had landed on the cradle as she made her way to the wardrobe.

'The flowers are simply magnificent,' she heard her mother say behind her. 'Don't you think so, dear?'

She grunted something in response as she dragged on a pair of jeans, pulling off the robe and throwing on a T-shirt and zipper jacket, slipping her feet into moccasins.

'Mackenzi,' her mother called. 'What are you doing? The wedding…'

She turned then, barely able to see anyone through a fog of tears. 'I don't think there's going to be a wedding.' And she fled.

'What do you mean, she's gone?' Dante's gut clenched down in panic. 'Where?'

'We don't know,' Mackenzi's mother said. 'She just rushed out of here like the devil was at her heels. And Dante?'

'Yes?'

'She said she didn't think there was going to be a wedding.'

He put down the receiver and roared his frustration. What had happened to make her take off like that? There'd been no indication, no clue that she was feeling disgruntled, quite the reverse. In fact, he'd never seen her happier than the last few days leading up to the wedding. What on earth had gone wrong?

'Anything wrong?' He turned to see Adrian letting himself into the room with their buttonholes.

'It's Mackenzi,' he said, jabbing numbers into the phone. 'She's gone.'

'Gone?' he said, putting the flowers down on the coffee-table and pouring himself a shot of whiskey. 'You mean she's changed her mind?'

'I don't know,' Dante said, frowning when he glanced at the time. 'Not until I talk to her. *Pick up. Pick up,*' he urged the other end.

'Maybe it's for the best,' Adrian conjectured, tossing back his whiskey in one neat action, baring his teeth as it hit the spot. 'Maybe you're better to find out how flaky she is now, before you tie the knot.'

'Shut up, Adrian.' The phone picked up. 'Natalie! Is that you? Have you seen Mackenzi?'

'Isn't she in her room? She called from there a little while ago?'

'What did she want?'

'It was really strange. She just asked if the hotel was closing. I thought it was odd she didn't seem to know...'

Oh my God! 'And what did you tell her?'

'Just that it was. She didn't give me a chance to say anything else.'

Could it be any worse? He thanked her and hung up in the space of less than a second, reaching for his car keys the next.

'Where are you going?' asked Adrian, already pouring his second whiskey.

'To find her.'

'Are you sure she's worth it? You could do better than some slapper who exchanges sex for favours.'

Dante had picked him up and slammed him up against the bureau before Adrian knew what had hit him, his glass of whiskey flinging contents in a sweeping golden arc around the room before tumbling down onto the carpet. 'You don't know anything about her!' he said, regretting the moment on the plane when he'd trusted Adrian enough to share the secret of their intimate deal. And now Mackenzi was missing. Coincidence?

'What do you know about Mackenzi running away?'

Adrian's arms flailed helplessly as he shook his head. 'Me, boss? Nothing.'

Dante snarled at him, smelling his fear, knowing he was lying. 'Whatever possessed me to think you'd ever make a best man?' He pulled him suddenly towards him and gave him a shove sideways that sent him tumbling into the sofa. 'I want you out of here by the time I get back. And I never want to see you again.'

'But boss—'

'Never!'

He powered the car out of the driveway, turning onto the tangled hills road on a hunch, hoping he was right. He had to find her. He had to bring her back.

But the roads looked different from the last time he'd followed her; the fog had cleared away, the views over the surrounding hills were long and everything looked different. Every last thing.

She must have left the hotel in a complete state. God, if anything had happened to her! If anything had happened before he had the chance to tell her.

He thumped the heel of his hand on the steering wheel. Why had it taken him so long to realize? Adrian was so far off the mark, and yet it had been like a wake-up call, forcing him to realize what she meant to him. She was no slapper ready to exchange sex for favours, he knew that now.

She was a passionate, vibrant woman.

The mother of his child.

The woman he loved!

He shot past the turnoff before he'd realized, cursing as he had to double back, hoping it was the turnoff he needed.

But was it already too late?

Misty met her at the door, winding her way around her legs, pretending it was dinner time already like she always did, even though it was barely midday. Mackenzi reached down and picked her up, stroking her as she let herself into her house.

'You might love me for my cat food, but at least you love me,' she said, feeling a fresh batch of tears welling up and pressing to be launched. She forced the feeling back. She would not cry. Damn Dante Carrazzo to hell and back, but she would not cry!

She put the cat down on the back of the sofa and went to her room. She'd left her better suitcase back at the hotel, but she had an older, dustier one on top of her wardrobe. She stood on a chair and pulled it down, blowing off the fine coating of dust before setting it down on her bed. She'd go away somewhere. She didn't know where, but somewhere nobody could find her.

Especially if nobody's name was Dante Carrazzo.

The phone rang and she jumped at the sound, but she didn't answer it. It was better if people didn't know where she was. She'd call her parents later, when she'd found herself a bolthole. She'd tell them she was sorry but it had been a mistake. She'd tell them she'd be okay. And somehow—*somehow*—she'd make them believe it.

She tossed the last of her clothes in, not overly concerned what was there, and zipped the bag up, remembering the trouble she'd had last time when she'd packed to leave this house. No such difficulty this time. Wherever she was going, she wasn't out to impress.

Mackenzi was just lugging the suitcase down the hallway when she heard it—the powerful engine roaring closer, and the spew of gravel as it pulled to a screeching stop outside. A feeling of *déjà vu* cementing her insides. *Dante!* She turned, fleeing the other way down her hallway even as she heard the sound of a car door slamming and running footsteps up the path. She didn't want to see him, didn't want to listen to any more lies. Didn't want him to know how much he'd hurt her.

Because she was under no misconception why he was here. It wasn't for her sake. It was because he wanted their baby. That was when this whole marriage idea had arisen. It had never had anything to do with her. And she'd tried to convince herself that he loved her.

Fool!

Her front door flew open. 'Mackenzi!'

She stiffened and turned slowly, watching him come closer, feeling like a rabbit caught in the headlights. 'Go away!'

'You have to listen to me.'

'No! I'm done with listening to you. You lied to me. You did before, you will again.'

'Mackenzi, please?'

'Get out of my way. I'd like to leave now.'

'I can't let you do that, not like this, not before you give me a chance to explain.'

She gave up trying to move anywhere down the corridor and fled into the relative space of her living room, aware he would follow her, knowing the second he did. Misty looked up warily as the warring factions drew nearer, the end of her tail flicking dangerously. 'I told you, I don't want to hear it! We had a deal and you broke it.'

'I didn't break it.'

'You damned well did. You promised me you'd save Ashton House and I believed you. But you're closing it. Adrian told me you'd already decided.'

Dante cursed out loud. 'Adrian is a malicious bastard. He's toxic. I've told him to clear out.'

'Oh, does that mean you got rid of Natalie too? Because she said the same thing. Don't try to blame Adrian for your failings, Dante, because I'm over it. I'm over everything, as of right now.'

He sighed then and she almost thought he was conceding defeat, his expression softening so markedly. 'I wanted it to be a surprise,' he told her, his tone almost imploring.

'What—that you'd decided to pull Ashton House down after all? I just bet you wanted it to be a surprise.' But her tone was less savage than she'd intended, his change of mood throwing her off-balance.

He shook his head. 'I'm not closing it to pull it down.'

She tilted her head. 'But you *are* closing it?'

'Yes.'

'But why? We had a deal. You promised me you'd save Ashton House. You promised! And I don't matter to you.

This baby doesn't matter to you. No matter what you say or what you promise, all you're interested in doing is in pulling Sara and Jonas Douglas down.'

He covered his upturned face with his hands, but it couldn't mask the agonized roar that sent chills down Mackenzi's spine and had Misty fleeing from the room.

'Yes,' he said, his eyes wild in his flushed face, his neck corded and tight. 'That *was* all I wanted. To pull them down. To make them pay for what they'd done.'

More chills descended her spine, ripping her throat of voice, leaving her only with a croaking whisper. She wrapped her arms around her midriff. 'What did they do?'

He shook his head, his eyes closed, raking one hand through his hair. Then he opened his eyes.

'Mackenzi,' he said softly, looking suddenly exhausted, gesturing to the sofa. 'I have to tell you something. Maybe something I should have told you a long time ago. But something I need to tell you if only you'll understand. Will you hear me out?'

She stood there uncertainly, not knowing if she wanted to listen, knowing she couldn't listen if it meant hearing more lies.

He smiled, if it could have been called that, crooked and halfway resigned. 'Please,' he insisted. 'It's important.'

She nodded briefly and sat down on the sofa, thinking that maybe something in what he had to say would make some sense out of what had happened, realising it was important that for once he wanted to open up about the past.

'I never knew my parents,' he started. 'My mother was young, of Italian descent, apparently. My father I have no knowledge of, but he was probably young too. But her family were ashamed and put me in foster care, preferring someone else to take care of their mistake, and to preserve the worth of their daughter.'

'Dante,' she said, her heart going out to him. A child no one had wanted, so different from her own conception where her parents had been so desperate to have a child they'd almost bankrupted themselves in the process. 'I had no idea.'

'There's more,' he said. 'When I was barely two years old a family came to see me. They were professional people, older and both workaholics, but they'd had a child late in life, a boy the same age as me.'

Her skin prickled. 'You don't mean Sara and Jonas?'

He flicked her a look that told her she was right. 'They took me in to live with them.'

'But that can't be. The Douglas family had only two boys, Jake and—' cold shivers descended her spine as she put two and two together '—Danny. *Daniel Douglas*,' she whispered, her mind fixing the pieces together, latching onto the truth while her eyes searched his face. She tried to remember the old photos she'd seen, tried to see the similarity. 'Jake was the brother killed in a car accident, but Danny disappeared without trace.'

He looked down at her, his expression bleak, and she saw something akin to pain flash through his eyes.

'You're Danny, aren't you?'

He looked bereft and she wanted to reach out and comfort him, to take him in her arms and cradle him, this man who had been a boy unwanted. But he hadn't been totally unwanted—he'd been taken in by one of the wealthiest families around.

'Sara and Jonas adopted you. And yet this is the way you repay them? I don't understand.'

'They didn't adopt me!' he shouted, jumping to his feet, holding his hands upside down like claws. 'They *harvested* me! They chose a child the same age as theirs for the sole purpose of giving their progeny a playmate, a diversion, a distraction. Someone that would keep him company when Sara and Jonas weren't there. Because they were *never* there.

'I used to wonder why it was that we never had sleep-overs with friends, never were allowed to join school sports teams. We were closeted in the grounds before and after school. And I was there solely to keep Jake amused.'

She was shaking her head. 'But that's so cold-blooded. It's too horrible. Surely nobody could do that to a child—to children?'

'I wanted to think that too. I knew they were busy. They were making millions. And I had been selected to live in the lap of luxury after being rescued from foster-care ob-scurity. Who was I to complain?'

He trailed off, and in the ensuing quiet Misty ventured back into the room, curling her way around Mackenzi's legs before exploring further, sniffing out their visitor warily before getting too close. 'So what happened?'

'It was Jake's seventeenth birthday,' he said. 'His birthday was two months before mine and there was a big party. They'd given him a Porsche, and we couldn't wait to take it for a spin, but we had the party to get through first. We couldn't wait.

'But, before the party was over, Sara and Jonas called me into their office. It seemed odd, though at the time I wondered if they just wanted to find out what I'd like for my birthday, or whether it had to do with the trip overseas we'd both planned together at the end of the year. I wasn't worried about the cars; thrill-seeking was always Jake's get-out. He was always my hero, the big brother, the risk-taker. Always the thrill-seeker.'

'And what about you? What were you like?'

He looked at her, his eyes misty with remembrance. 'I had dreams. I was fascinated by what Sara and Jonas had achieved. I used to listen to them talking late at night when I was supposed to be in bed, talking about property and rates of return and discounted cash-flows. I longed to go to the university they'd tried to talk Jake into and study business and be just like them.'

'Then why did you disappear?'

He gave a sad laugh. 'I didn't exactly "disappear". On that night, the night of Jake's birthday party, they told me. They didn't need me any more, they both said. I'd served my purpose and it was time for me to go.'

'They threw you out?'

'That very night. They gave me a cheque for ten-thousand dollars and told me not to bother to say goodbye to Jake, because he knew and he didn't care, but just to get out of their lives.'

'They did that to you?'

He nodded. 'But not before telling me my real name wasn't Daniel Douglas, as I'd grown up believing, but Dante Carrazzo. To preserve my heritage, they told me that night—but I know it was so that I could have no claim on them, no link, no connection by name with the family that had taken me in only to cast me out when my purpose was fulfilled.'

'And so you left.'

'I had money,' he said. 'The money they'd given me. And I had a passport they'd applied for in my real name, using a photograph intended for the passport that I thought I was applying for to accompany Jake.

'So I took the money. I was so shellshocked I took the money and left that night, and never saw them again. But I didn't blow the money like I'm sure they were convinced I would. I didn't end up fading into obscurity like they would have hoped. I bought a one-way ticket to London, finding a job as a clerk in a real-estate business, looking after plumbing callouts and rental short-payments and gradually working my way up through the ranks until I could start my own business.'

'No wonder it seemed like you'd come from nowhere. And you never got to go to university?'

He gave a wan smile as Misty started patrolling his legs, first carefully around the perimeter, before venturing in between, curving her spine up around his shins.

'No. And maybe I should be grateful to Sara and Jonas for that. Because I'm sure I learned one hell of a lot more doing property boot-camp. I know they must have been surprised by how much I learned. I broke out and started my own property-management business, adding investment and property-development strings to my bow.'

'You used that strength to get back at them.'

'I did,' he said, without a trace of noticeable remorse. 'I'd been in my first job two years when I learned that Jake had died three months before, and then only through a tiny article on the newspaper wrapped around my takeaway fish and chips. I couldn't believe it. Jake had been the chosen one, the heir, he'd been given everything he wanted and more, and yet it hadn't done him any good. And they'd never let me say goodbye. I should have said goodbye. I know he never would have wanted me to leave.'

He took a deep breath. 'And it was then that I decided that I'd make them pay—for Jake, for me, for the parents they'd made out they were and yet had never been.'

'And so you set out to destroy them.'

He smiled then. 'It took a while. They were streets ahead of me, but with time I gradually caught up, especially once Jonas started gambling. It must have blown them away when they found out who it was who'd come courting. I often wondered about that, and whether they'd spill the beans to the press and tell them who I really was.' He looked at her, his eyebrows raised. 'But they couldn't, could they? Not without revealing the whole sorry story. And who would possibly feel sorry for them then?'

Mackenzi was speechless for what seemed like minutes, the ticking of her ancient mantel clock the only noise—that and Misty's purr as she settled on Dante's lap and pushed her head into his large hand, almost as if she sensed that right now Dante needed something physical, something real, to mend the pain.

'It's horrible,' she said at last. 'I had no idea. They always seemed such nice people.'

He shrugged. 'Maybe they were. They just should never have had children.'

'So that's what you have against Ashton House,' she whispered. 'Their final holding, the star in their crown.'

He gave a hard, grating laugh. 'Oh yes. Not to mention it was the site of Jake's seventeenth-birthday party.'

She looked at him in horror, suddenly realising the full depth of his abhorrence. 'Oh my God,' she said, unable to sit down any longer, reaching out a hand to his. 'No wonder you hate it so much. No wonder you can't wait to see it torn down.'

He shrugged and smiled strangely. 'It used to seem important, but just lately it doesn't seem to matter so much.'

'But you're closing the hotel, you said that. Why would you do that?'

'It's true,' he said, leaning closer, collecting her other hand and enclosing them both in his own. 'You see, I had this idea. You kept telling me I should be building things and not destroying them, and I knew you wanted me to save the hotel. But the world has more than enough hotels, don't you think?'

She laughed a little too nervously, trying to keep up, unsure where he was going but appreciating the change in tone, the enthusiasm he was demonstrating. More than anything appreciating the warm of his skin against her own. 'So what did you have in mind?'

'This is probably crazy,' he admitted. 'God knows, Adrian tried to talk me out of it. But, when I think back on it, that first foster-family was the only family who ever really wanted me. They took me in and gave me a home and cared for me when no one else would. And for no other reason than because I needed it. And so, when you made me promise to keep Ashton House, I thought about turning it into a place where families could go—foster families, with kids who didn't belong anywhere or to anyone, but who'd been taken in anyway. To give them a break and a chance to breathe some fresh air and get a new outlook on life.' He looked at her expectantly.

She smiled. 'So that's why you're closing the hotel? So you can turn it into a respite-care centre for foster kids and their families?'

He was nodding. 'Yes. Would you mind? You made me promise not to close Ashton House, but you never said it had to stay a hotel. What do you think?'

'I think it's the most wonderful idea I've ever heard.'

His smile widened, his eyes glinting with pleasure. 'You do?'

'I'm so proud of you,' she said, throwing her arms around him. 'To go through what you've been through. I had no idea. I'm so sorry I didn't believe you when you promised to save Ashton House.'

He wrapped an arm around her shoulders, pulling her in tight. 'You were right not to believe me. I was determined to destroy it all along—I'd instructed Adrian to close the hotel even before you found out you were pregnant. But when you made that marriage ultimatum I finally had to look at what I had in mind. And suddenly it didn't matter any more. I tried, but I couldn't hang onto that hatred, and your words made sense to me—that I could build something, rather than destroy it.' He looked down at her and smiled. 'You taught me that, and I will never know how to thank you enough.'

She beamed up at him, suddenly biting her lip. 'I'm sorry I ran out on you today.'

'I'm not.' And when she frowned and pulled away he pulled her back. 'I didn't mean it like that. I meant that until today I didn't realize what you meant to me. I knew I liked having you around, and I had the bonus that you were carrying my child, but until today—until I thought I'd lost you forever—I never realized just how much you meant to me.'

Her heart jumped, skipped a beat and resumed again, louder than ever. 'You mean…?'

He smiled. 'I love you, Mackenzi Rose. I love you so much it almost killed me to think I'd lost you. Never do that to me again, promise?'

'Only if you promise never to scare the hell out of me with any of your surprises, okay? If you've got something good to tell me, please tell me.'

He laughed and squeezed her tighter. 'It's a deal.'

'And while we're on the subject of being honest…' She looked up at him and decided there were better ways than words. She wrapped her arms around his neck and kissed him, pouring every bit of herself and her love into it.

He growled when finally she withdrew. 'Does that mean what I think it means?'

She purred. 'It does. I love you, Dante Carrazzo. For now. And forever more.'

'Hmmm,' he said, moving into the next kiss. 'I like the sound of that.'

There was a rattling at the front door, a scrape and then the sound of rickety footsteps down the hallway. 'Oh, it's you,' Mrs Gepp said, finding them in the lounge. 'I heard a noise and thought I'd better come looking. I thought you were supposed to be off getting married.'

'I was,' she said, smiling. 'I mean, we are.'

'Goodness, girlie, you'd better get going then. So who's this, then—not the fellow you're marrying?'

Dante took her gnarled hand in his own. 'Dante Carrazzo, at your service.'

'Good,' she said, holding on tight and pulling him down to her height like she was confiding in him. 'Then you're just the person I want to talk to. I get worried the time Mack puts into her job. She's always working late and sleeping over. I can't count the number of times she's rung me to say she's not coming home and asking if I can feed Misty for her. She needs a real reason to come home. She needs a man to set her straight about what's important in life. I know she won't listen to me—'

Mackenzi cut her off with a nervous laugh. 'Thanks, Mrs Gepp, I guess we'd better be getting back to the wedding. You sure you won't join us? You're more than welcome, you know.'

'Not with this dodgy hip,' she complained, nursing her side. 'Besides, weddings always make me cry. Not a good look when you're pushing eighty-five or so. You two run along now.'

Mackenzi dipped to give her a kiss and a quick squeeze. 'Thanks for everything, Mrs Gepp.'

'One more thing!' she yelled out as they ran for Dante's car. 'I always thought it was bad luck for the groom to see the bride before the wedding.'

Dante looked at Mackenzi and smiled. 'Not this time,' he said.

Barely at the end of the driveway, he suddenly braked the car to a stop and switched off the ignition. Then he turned to his bride-to-be, his eyes dark with self-recrimination. 'You frequently stayed overnight at the hotel. Mrs Gepp said so.'

'If I was working late, sure. It didn't make sense to drive all the way home if it was really late or if the weather was bad.'

There was a too-long pause. 'Like the night I arrived.'

She stole a lungful of air, hung onto it and then let it go in a rush. Because, in the scheme of things, the past didn't matter. She loved this man. The past meant nothing any more, except for whatever demons Dante still had left to put to rest. She gave a brief nod. 'Yes. Exactly like the night you arrived.'

'You weren't waiting for me at all that night,' he said. 'You weren't lying in wait to seduce me. Like you told me before, you were merely making use of a vacant bed. I didn't believe you.'

She looked away. She'd given him every reason to think what he had, but still the memory of that night's disappointment—the fact he'd written her off so easily and accused her of being little more than a whore—was surprisingly still all too real. Looking over the gum-tree-studded hills around them, she said, 'I worked late that night preparing the projections for you in preparation for your visit. And, with the Melbourne airports closed with the weather, nobody figured you'd get there until at least breakfast. I thought you'd never know if I borrowed your bed for a few hours.' She shrugged as she turned back. 'Nobody expected you'd drive instead. Nobody realized what it meant to you.'

He touched a hand to her neck, cupping her ear. 'And I never even bothered to look at those projections.'

She swallowed, feeling her colour rising, sending him a shaky smile—thinking he'd got a look at far more that night than he'd bargained for. 'Those reports are irrelevant now that you've decided on a different course. Whatever I prepared for the hotel, it doesn't matter, not now you have something better planned.'

He frowned. 'I accused you of orchestrating the whole situation. I was so wrong. And I was wrong to take advantage of you, to assume you were no more than a wh—'

'Oh no,' she said, stopping him with a hand to his lips. 'It doesn't matter now. You didn't take advantage of me. You didn't.'

He looked away. 'But I gave you no choice.'

She grabbed hold of his jaw and yanked it around until he faced her. 'I had a choice. Yes, I was surprised to find you turn up that night. I was shocked and blown away to find a naked stranger making moves on me—but I had a clear choice. I could have screamed blue murder when I came to. I could have fled from that bed right then and there.'

His eyes creased at the corners. 'But you didn't. And that would be because…?'

She let her hand slide from his jaw and screwed round ninety degrees in her seat. There were some things she couldn't admit face to face. 'For me,' she said. 'Because I didn't want you to stop.'

There was hushed silence in the car.

'Why did you let me do that to you, to put you in that position?'

She looked out the windscreen at gum-tree tops amid blue sky and gave a wan smile. 'Because nobody had ever made me feel as good as you had, awake or asleep. And, even when I'd woken up and realized who you were, and knew I was risking everything, I couldn't stop myself. I couldn't say no. I wanted to feel more.'

'You thought I was your ex-boyfriend.'

'If I did it was only because I felt so different to how I

felt with him! He'd always told me that I was an ice queen, unfeeling and cold.' She instinctively hugged her arms around herself and, like a weighted pendulum, started to rock forward in her seat.

His arms came around her like a vice, dragging her off course and against him instead. 'He was an idiot.'

She tried to smile. Tried and failed miserably. 'He knew I was an IVF baby. He told me that's why I couldn't feel anything with him,' she said. 'Because I wasn't a real woman. Because I'd been *manufactured*.'

Dante sighed roughly and hugged her closer. He wanted to kill the bastard. He pressed his lips to her hair. 'You couldn't have believed him?'

She tightened in his arms but she didn't pull away. 'You think I wanted to? But in a way it made sense. Maybe I was frigid. Because I'd never found someone who made me feel like a woman, who made me want to have sex.' She tilted her head up towards him. 'Not until you—and that night.'

If the moon had been out, he would have howled at it. She was his woman and his alone, and his heart was so swollen it threatened to burst from his chest.

He lifted her hands in his, pressing the backs of them to his mouth. 'Listen to me, and believe it—you are the hottest woman I've ever known, and you are a real woman in every sense of the word.'

She smiled back at him. 'I used to have a dream lover who visited me some nights. I think he was trying to tell me that.'

He tilted her chin up and focused on her lips. 'You don't need a dream lover any more.'

'No,' she agreed, her lips dancing enticingly under his. 'Now I've got the real thing.'

They were only a couple of hours late for the wedding and nobody seemed to mind. At her neck she wore the emerald necklace, the matching earrings swaying in time as she walked. Dante had kept them for her, knowing they were perfect for her, knowing the time was right. He'd presented them to her before the ceremony as his wedding gift, a token of his love, and Mackenzi had accepted them, knowing it was true.

Stuart Quinn had happily agreed to act as best man and stood alongside Dante, his sun-and-salt-battered features beaming with pride. But it was Dante who drew her eye as her father led her down the blossom-lined walkway to the outdoor altar. Dante whose eyes smouldered with a rare emotion that drew her towards him like a magnet. Dante, whose slightly upturned lips spoke volumes as she came closer.

'You always told me the view from here was beautiful,' he whispered, taking her arm in his and looking her in the eyes as she drew alongside him. 'But this view is the very best. I love you, Mackenzi.'

She looked back at him and felt his love embrace her, wrapping around her, warm and real. 'As I love you, Dante. Forever.'

And then he dipped his head and kissed her. Deeply. Thoroughly. Shamelessly.

Thunderous applause broke out behind them, but it was only the polite coughing of the celebrant that finally brought about an end to the kiss.

'Most unconventional,' he said, his broad smile at odds with the shaking of his head. 'But perhaps now we can get this show on the road.'

He looked over his Bible to the gathering of guests. 'Dearly beloved…'

HARLEQUIN Presents

Undressed
BY THE BOSS

From sensible suits…into satin sheets!

Stranded in a Nevada hotel, Kate throws herself
on the mercy of hotelier Zack Boudreaux.
In exchange for a job and a way home, he'll
make her his very personal assistant….

THE TYCOON'S VERY
PERSONAL ASSISTANT
by Heidi Rice

Book # 2761

Available in September:

If you love stories about a gorgeous boss, look out for:

BUSINESS IN THE
BEDROOM
by Anne Oliver

Book # 2770

Available next month in Harlequin Presents.

She's his in the bedroom, but he can't buy her love.

Billionaire and maharaja's heir Jay hired interior designer
Keira but began to think she was the
worst kind of wanton. Until he discovered—
firsthand—that she was a virgin...

Showered with diamonds, draped in exquisite lingerie,
whisked around the world...

**The ultimate fantasy becomes a reality
in Harlequin Presents**

VIRGIN FOR THE BILLIONAIRE'S TAKING
by Penny Jordan
Book #2755

Available in September:

HARLEQUIN® Presents®

THE SICILIANS

They seek passion—at any price!

Three Sicilians of aristocratic birth—with
revenge in mind and romance in their destinies!

Darci intends to teach legendary womanizer
Luc Gambrelli a lesson—but as soon as
the smolderingly handsome Sicilian film
producer turns the tables on her, the game
begins to get dirty....

THE SICILIAN'S
INNOCENT MISTRESS

The third book in this sizzling trilogy by

Carole Mortimer

Book #2758

Available in September

REQUEST YOUR FREE BOOKS!

2 FREE NOVELS
PLUS 2
FREE GIFTS!

YES! Please send me 2 FREE Harlequin Presents® novels and my 2 FREE gifts (gifts are worth about $10). After receiving them, if I don't wish to receive any more books, I can return the shipping statement marked "cancel". If I don't cancel, I will receive 6 brand-new novels every month and be billed just $4.05 per book in the U.S. or $4.74 per book in Canada, plus 25¢ shipping and handling per book and applicable taxes, if any*. That's a savings of close to 15% off the cover price! I understand that accepting the 2 free books and gifts places me under no obligation to buy anything. I can always return a shipment and cancel at any time. Even if I never buy another book, the two free books and gifts are mine to keep forever.   106 HDN ERRW 306 HDN ERRL

Name _____ (PLEASE PRINT) _____

Address _____ Apt. # _____

City _____ State/Prov. _____ Zip/Postal Code _____

Signature (if under 18, a parent or guardian must sign)

Mail to the **Harlequin Reader Service:**
IN U.S.A.: P.O. Box 1867, Buffalo, NY 14240-1867
IN CANADA: P.O. Box 609, Fort Erie, Ontario L2A 5X3

Not valid to current subscribers of Harlequin Presents books.

Want to try two free books from another line?
Call 1-800-873-8635 or visit www.morefreebooks.com.

* Terms and prices subject to change without notice. N.Y. residents add applicable sales tax. Canadian residents will be charged applicable provincial taxes and GST. Offer not valid in Quebec. This offer is limited to one order per household. All orders subject to approval. Credit or debit balances in a customer's account(s) may be offset by any other outstanding balance owed by or to the customer. Please allow 4 to 6 weeks for delivery. Offer available while quantities last.

Your Privacy: Harlequin Books is committed to protecting your privacy. Our Privacy Policy is available online at www.eHarlequin.com or upon request from the Reader Service. From time to time we make our lists of customers available to reputable third parties who may have a product or service of interest to you. If you would prefer we not share your name and address, please check here. ☐

HP08R

SPECIAL EDITION™

NEW YORK TIMES BESTSELLING AUTHOR

DIANA PALMER

A brand-new Long, Tall Texans novel

HEART OF STONE

Feeling unwanted and unloved, Keely returns to Jacobsville and to Boone Sinclair, a rancher troubled by his own past. Boone has always seemed reserved, but now Keely discovers a sensuality with him that quickly turns to love. Can they each see past their own scars to let love in?

*Available September 2008
wherever you buy books.*

HARLEQUIN *Presents*

EXTRA

AN INNOCENT IN HIS BED

He's a man who takes whatever he pleases—even if it means bedding an inexperienced young woman....

With his intense good looks, commanding presence and unquestionable power, he'll carefully charm her and entice her into his bed, where he'll teach her the ways of love—by giving her the most amazingly sensual night of her life!

Don't miss any of the exciting stories in September:

#21 THE CATTLE BARON'S VIRGIN WIFE
by LINDSAY ARMSTRONG

#22 THE GREEK TYCOON'S INNOCENT MISTRESS
by KATHRYN ROSS

#23 PREGNANT BY THE ITALIAN COUNT
by CHRISTINA HOLLIS

#24 ANGELO'S CAPTIVE VIRGIN
by INDIA GREY